BASED ON THE ORIGINAL CHARACTERS CREATED BY

JIM DAVIS

PAPERCUTZ ™

NEW YORK

GARFIELD & Co

GRAPHIC NOVELS AVAILABLE FROM PAPERCUTZ ™

GRAPHIC NOVEL #1
"FISH TO FRY"

GRAPHIC NOVEL #2
"THE CURSE OF
THE CAT PEOPLE"

GRAPHIC NOVEL #3
"CATZILLA"

GRAPHIC NOVEL #4
"CAROLING CAPERS"

COMING SOON:

GRAPHIC NOVEL #5
"A GAME OF CAT
AND MOUSE"

GARFIELD & Co 4 - CAROLING CAPERS
"THE GARFIELD SHOW" SERIES © 2011- DARGAUD MEDIA.
ALL RIGHTS RESERVED. © PAWS. "GARFIELD" & GARFIELD
CHARACTERS ™ & © PAWS INC.- ALL RIGHTS RESERVED.
THE GARFIELD SHOW- A DARGAUD MEDIA PRODUCTION.
IN ASSOCIATION WITH FRANCE3 WITH THE PARTICIPATION
OF CENTRE NATIONAL DE LA CINÉMETAGRAPHIE AND THE
SUPPORT OF REGION LLE-DE-FRANCE. A SERIES DEVELOPED
BY PHILIPPE VIDAL, ROBERT REA & STEVE BALISSAT. BASED
UPON THE CHARACTERS CREATED BY JIM DAVIS. ORIGINAL
STORIES BY JULIEN MAGNAT (KING NERMAL, CAROLING
CAPERS, THE AMAZING FLYING DOG.)

CEDRIC MICHIELS - COMICS ADAPTATION
JOE JOHNSON - TRANSLATIONS
LEA HERNANDEZ - LETTERING
ADAM GRANO - PRODUCTION
MICHAEL PETRANEK - ASSOCIATE EDITOR
JIM SALICRUP
EDITOR-IN-CHIEF

ISBN: 978-1-59707-287-8

PRINTED IN CHINA
OCTOBER 2011 BY O.G. PRINTING PRODUCTIONS, LTD.
UNITS 2 & 3, 5/F, LEMMI CENTRE
50 HOI YUEN ROAD
KWON TONG, KOWLOON

DISTRIBUTED BY MACMILLAN
FIRST PAPERCUTZ PRINTING

GARFIELD & Co GRAPHIC NOVELS ARE AVAILABLE AT BOOK-
SELLERS EVERYWHERE IN HARDCOVER ONLY FOR $7.99 EACH.

OR ORDER FROM US - PLEASE ADD $4.00 FOR POSTAGE AND HANDLING FOR
THE FIRST BOOK, ADD $1.00 FOR EACH ADDITIONAL BOOK. PLEASE MAKE CHECK
PAYABLE TO: NBM PUBLISHING SEND TO: PAPERCUTZ, 40 EXCHANGE PLACE,
STE. 1308, NEW YORK, NY (1-800-886-1223)

WWW.PAPERCUTZ.COM

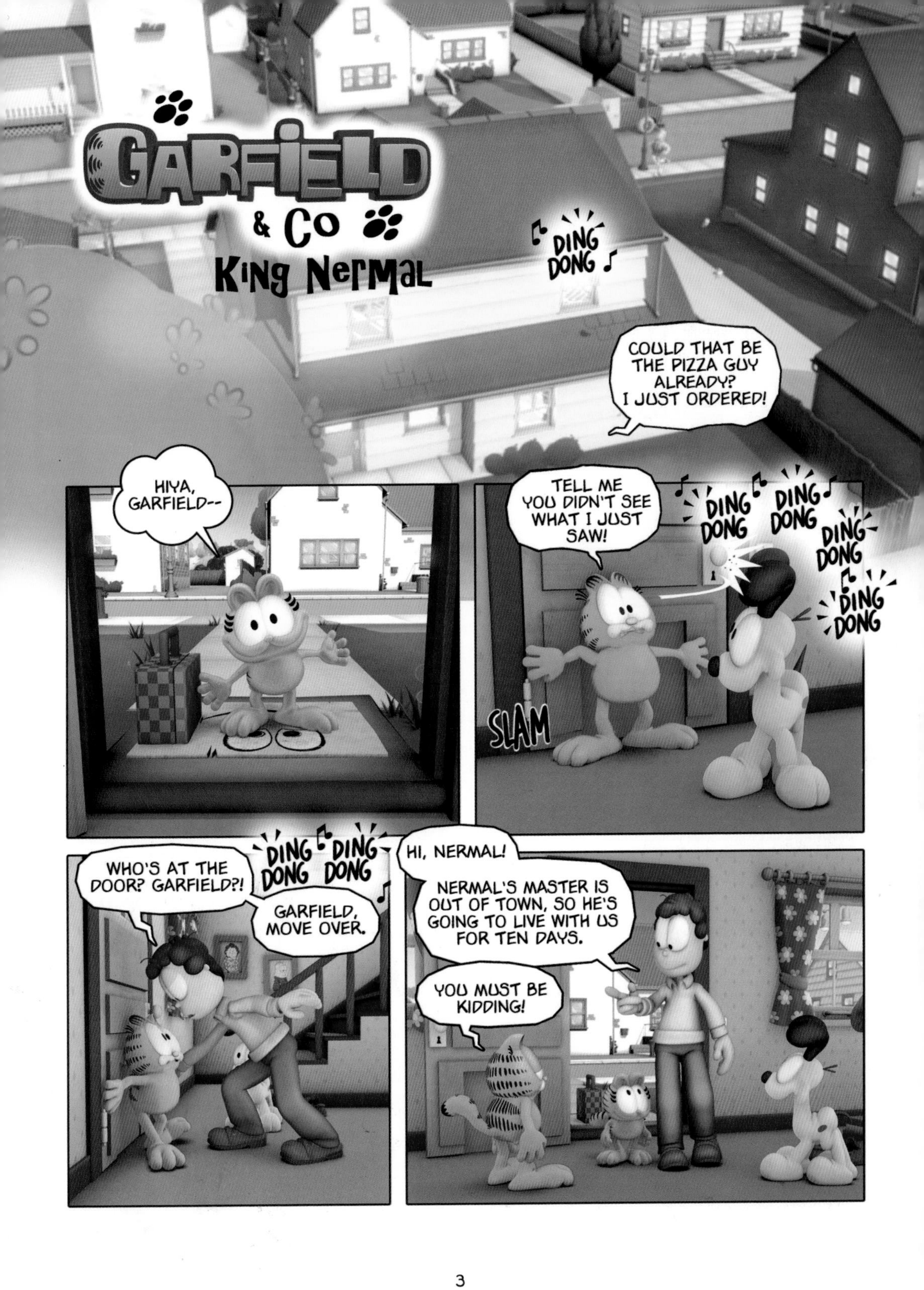
GARFIELD
& Co
King Nermal
DING DONG
COULD THAT BE THE PIZZA GUY ALREADY? I JUST ORDERED!
HIYA, GARFIELD--
TELL ME YOU DIDN'T SEE WHAT I JUST SAW!
DING DONG
DING DONG
DING DONG
DING DONG
SLAM
WHO'S AT THE DOOR? GARFIELD?!
DING DONG
DING DONG
GARFIELD, MOVE OVER.
HI, NERMAL!
NERMAL'S MASTER IS OUT OF TOWN, SO HE'S GOING TO LIVE WITH US FOR TEN DAYS.
YOU MUST BE KIDDING!

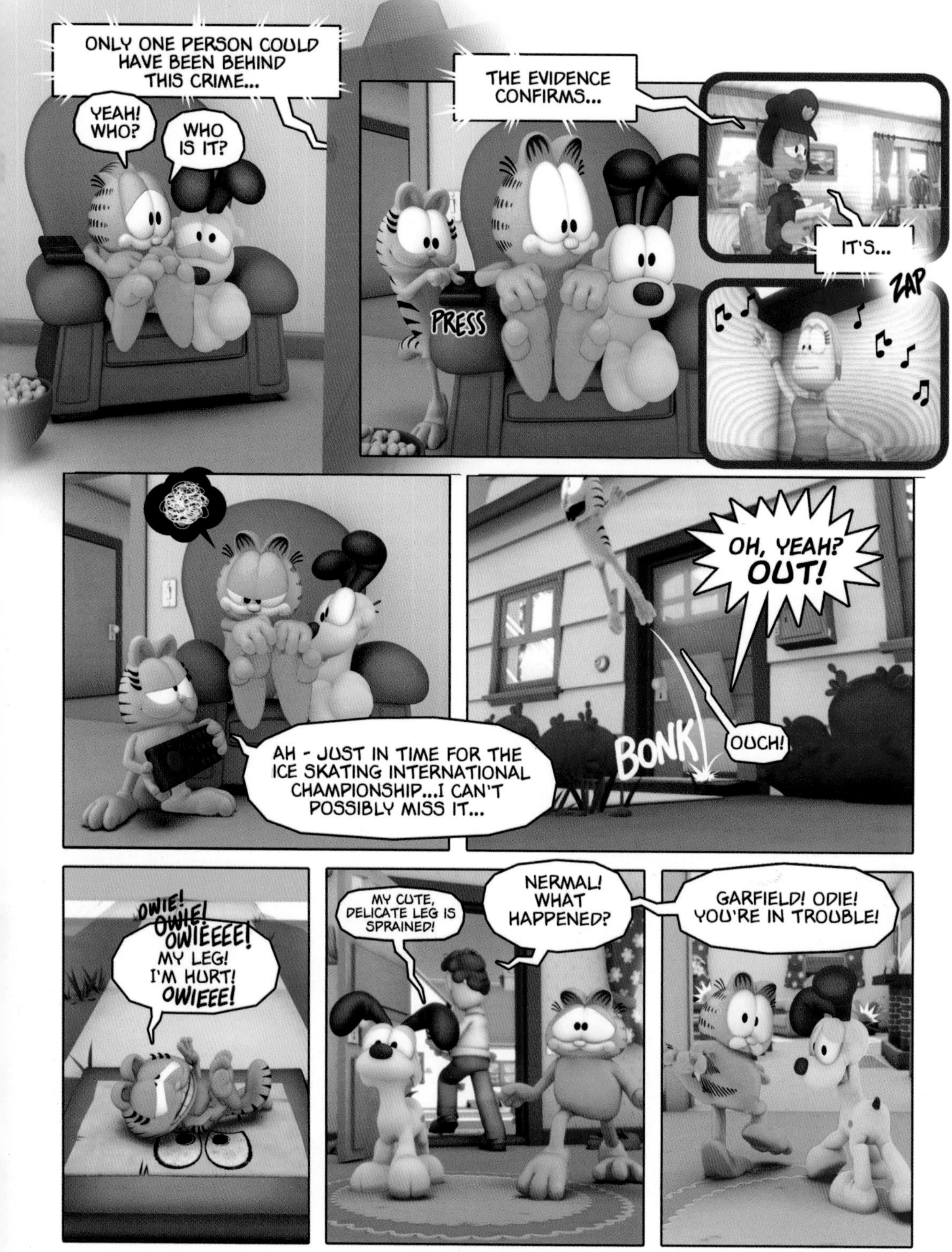
ONLY ONE PERSON COULD HAVE BEEN BEHIND THIS CRIME...
YEAH! WHO?
WHO IS IT?
THE EVIDENCE CONFIRMS...
PRESS
IT'S...
ZAP
AH - JUST IN TIME FOR THE ICE SKATING INTERNATIONAL CHAMPIONSHIP...I CAN'T POSSIBLY MISS IT...
OH, YEAH? OUT!
BONK
OUCH!
OWIE! OWIE! OWIEEEE! MY LEG! I'M HURT! OWIEEE!
MY CUTE, DELICATE LEG IS SPRAINED!
NERMAL! WHAT HAPPENED?
GARFIELD! ODIE! YOU'RE IN TROUBLE!

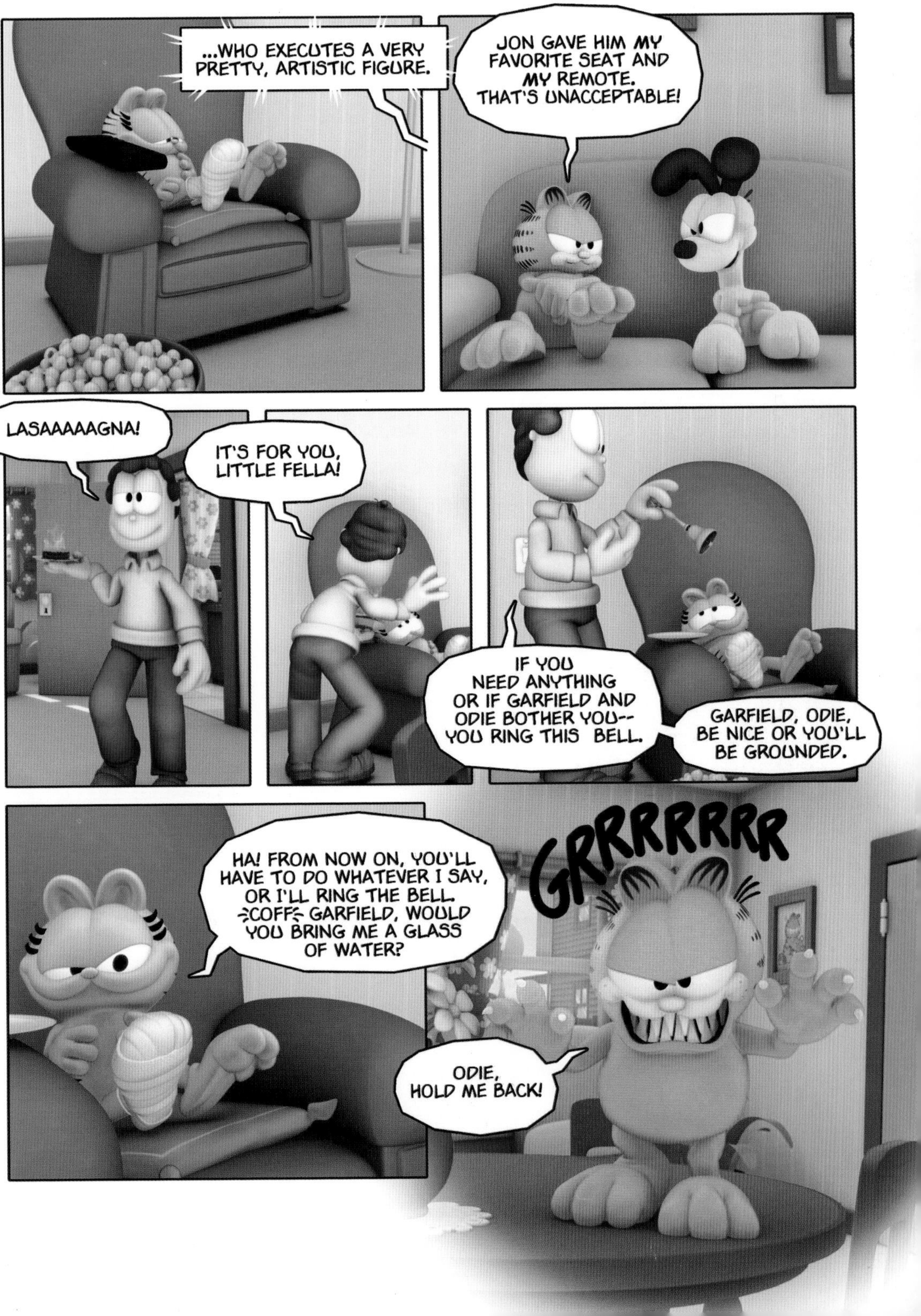
...WHO EXECUTES A VERY PRETTY, ARTISTIC FIGURE.
JON GAVE HIM MY FAVORITE SEAT AND MY REMOTE. THAT'S UNACCEPTABLE!
LASAAAAAGNA!
IT'S FOR YOU, LITTLE FELLA!
IF YOU NEED ANYTHING OR IF GARFIELD AND ODIE BOTHER YOU-- YOU RING THIS BELL.
GARFIELD, ODIE, BE NICE OR YOU'LL BE GROUNDED.
HA! FROM NOW ON, YOU'LL HAVE TO DO WHATEVER I SAY, OR I'LL RING THE BELL. COFF GARFIELD, WOULD YOU BRING ME A GLASS OF WATER?
GRRRRRRR
ODIE, HOLD ME BACK!

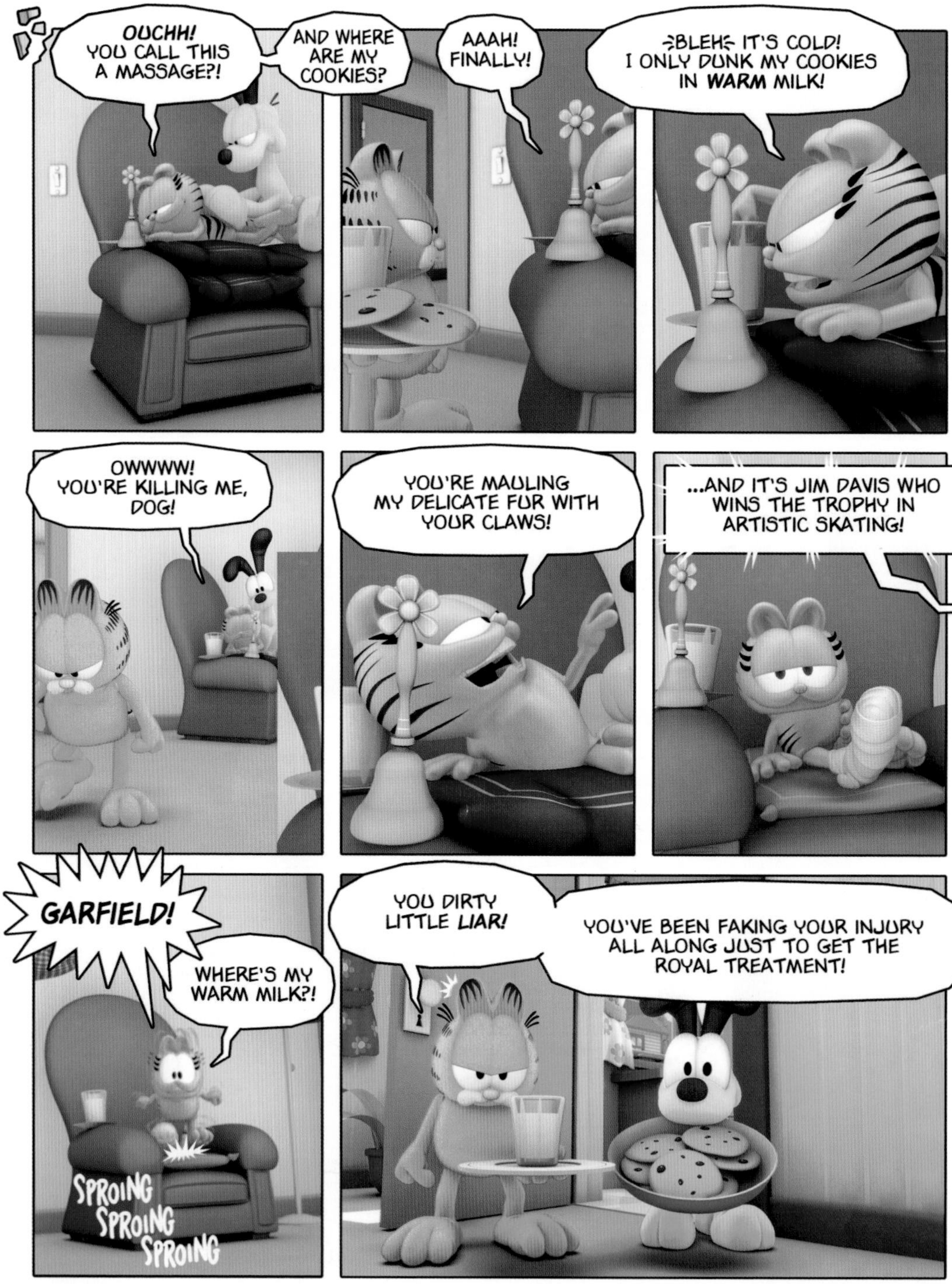
OUCHH! YOU CALL THIS A MASSAGE?!
AND WHERE ARE MY COOKIES?
AAAH! FINALLY!
BLEH IT'S COLD! I ONLY DUNK MY COOKIES IN WARM MILK!
OWWWW! YOU'RE KILLING ME, DOG!
YOU'RE MAULING MY DELICATE FUR WITH YOUR CLAWS!
...AND IT'S JIM DAVIS WHO WINS THE TROPHY IN ARTISTIC SKATING!
GARFIELD!
WHERE'S MY WARM MILK?!
SPROING SPROING SPROING
YOU DIRTY LITTLE LIAR!
YOU'VE BEEN FAKING YOUR INJURY ALL ALONG JUST TO GET THE ROYAL TREATMENT!

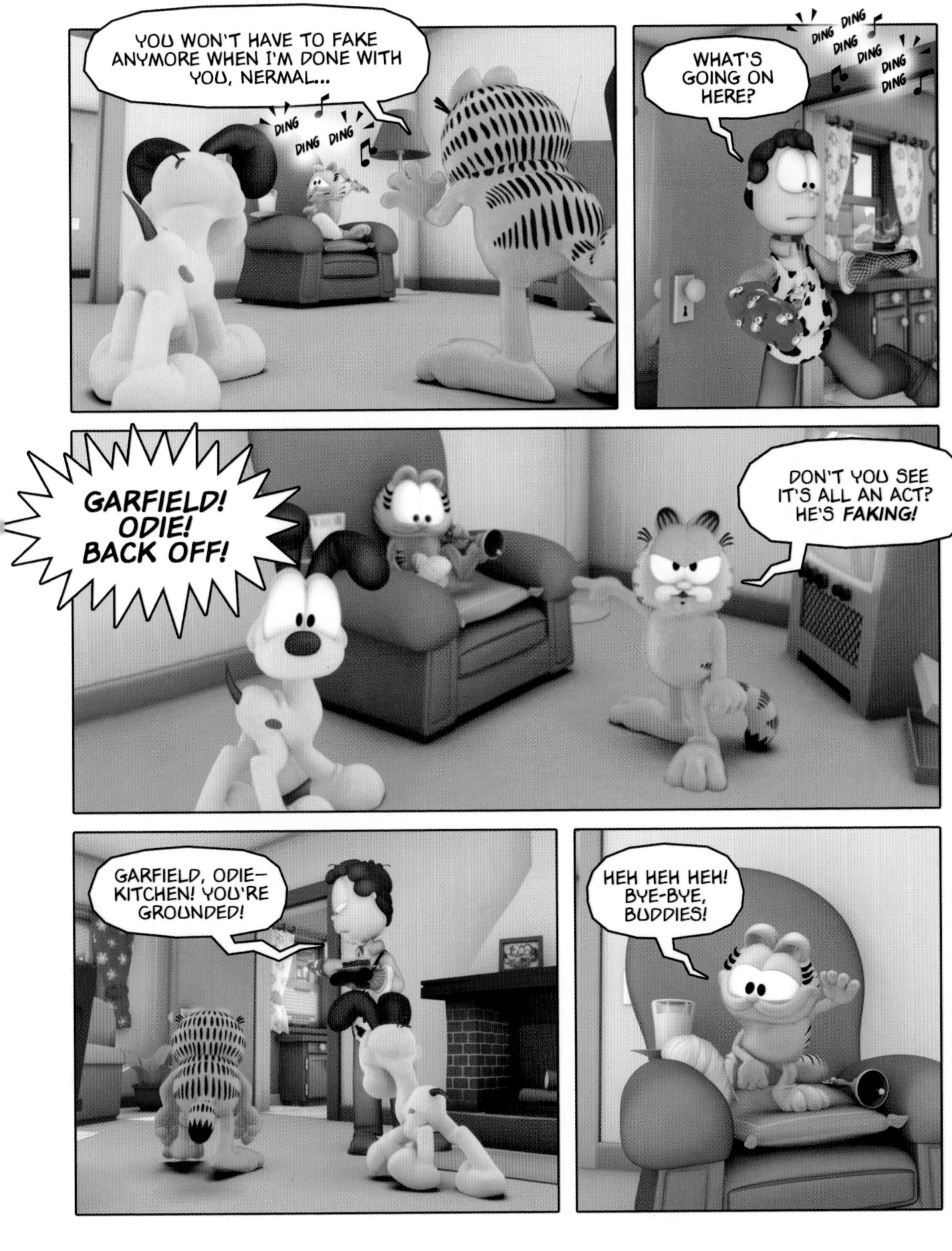

YOU WON'T HAVE TO FAKE ANYMORE WHEN I'M DONE WITH YOU, NERMAL...
DING DING DING
WHAT'S GOING ON HERE?
DING DING DING DING DING DING
GARFIELD! ODIE! BACK OFF!
DON'T YOU SEE IT'S ALL AN ACT? HE'S FAKING!
GARFIELD, ODIE-KITCHEN! YOU'RE GROUNDED!
HEH HEH HEH! BYE-BYE, BUDDIES!

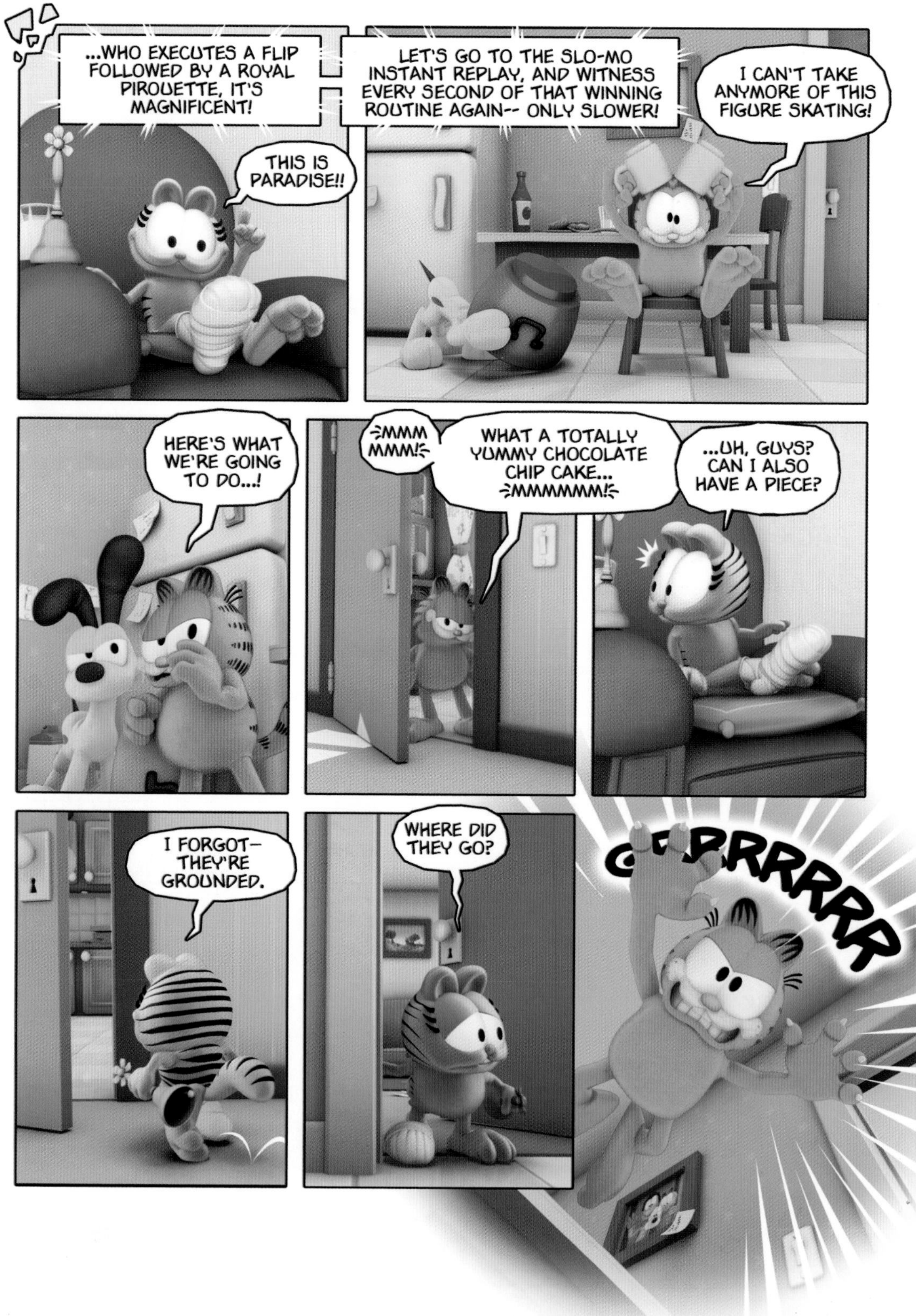
...WHO EXECUTES A FLIP FOLLOWED BY A ROYAL PIROUETTE, IT'S MAGNIFICENT!
THIS IS PARADISE!!
LET'S GO TO THE SLO-MO INSTANT REPLAY, AND WITNESS EVERY SECOND OF THAT WINNING ROUTINE AGAIN-- ONLY SLOWER!
I CAN'T TAKE ANYMORE OF THIS FIGURE SKATING!
HERE'S WHAT WE'RE GOING TO DO...!
MMM MMM!
WHAT A TOTALLY YUMMY CHOCOLATE CHIP CAKE... MMMMMM!
...UH, GUYS? CAN I ALSO HAVE A PIECE?
I FORGOT— THEY'RE GROUNDED.
WHERE DID THEY GO?
GRRRRRRR

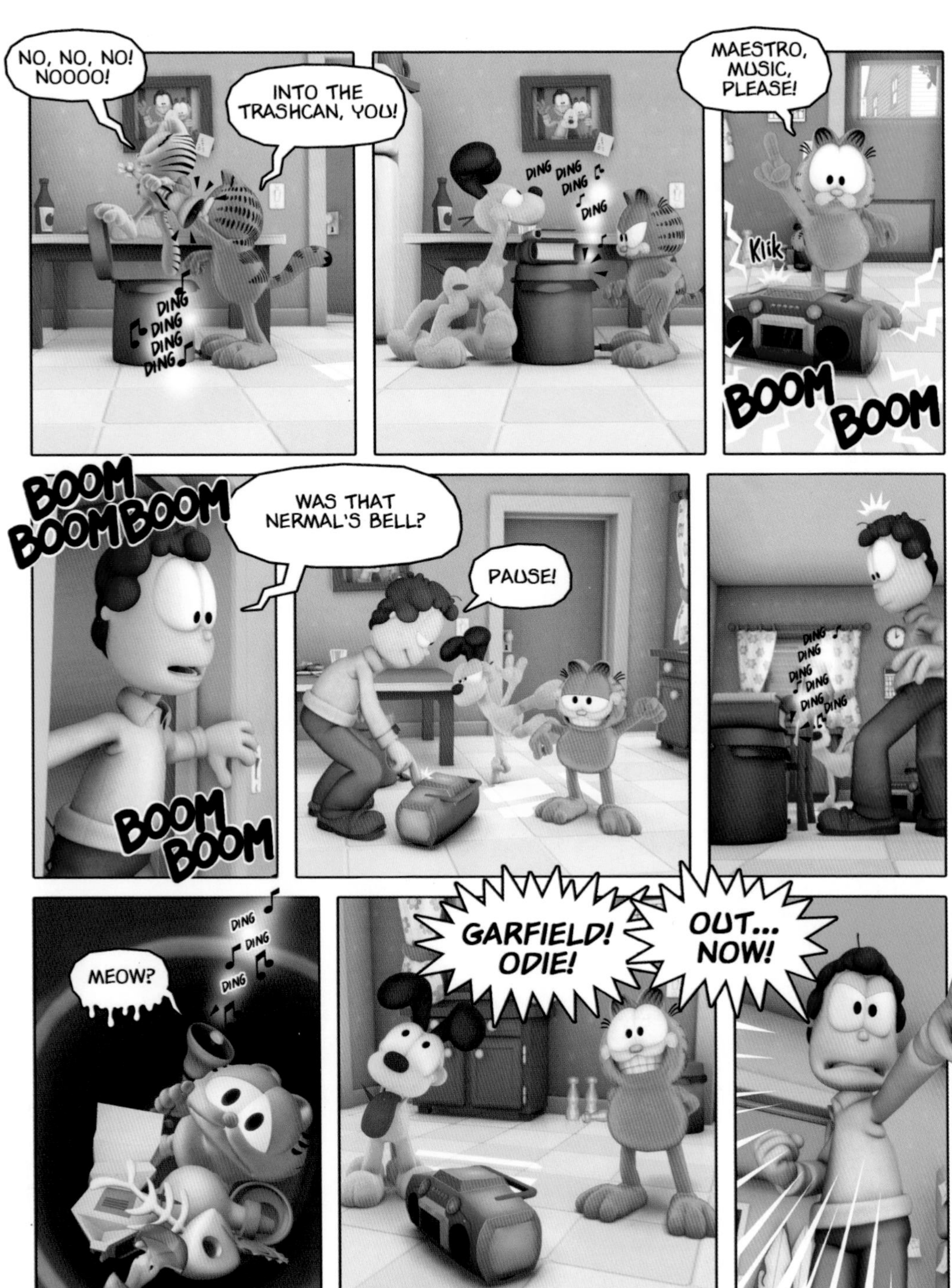
NO, NO, NO! NOOOO!
INTO THE TRASHCAN, YOU!
DING DING DING DING
DING DING DING DING
MAESTRO, MUSIC, PLEASE!
Klik
BOOM BOOM
BOOM BOOM BOOM
WAS THAT NERMAL'S BELL?
BOOM BOOM
PAUSE!
DING DING DING DING DING DING
DING DING DING
MEOW?
GARFIELD! ODIE!
OUT... NOW!

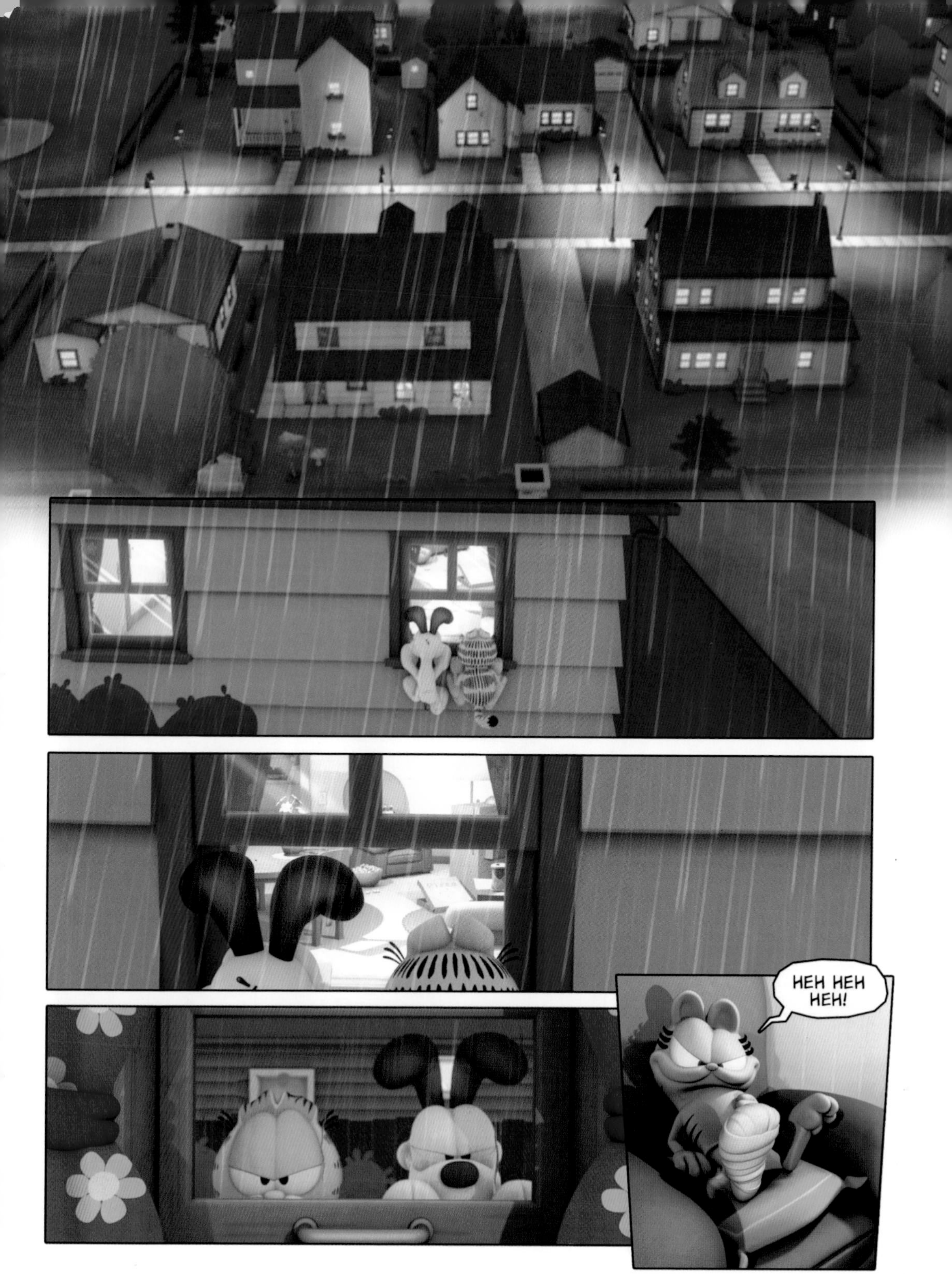
HEH HEH HEH!

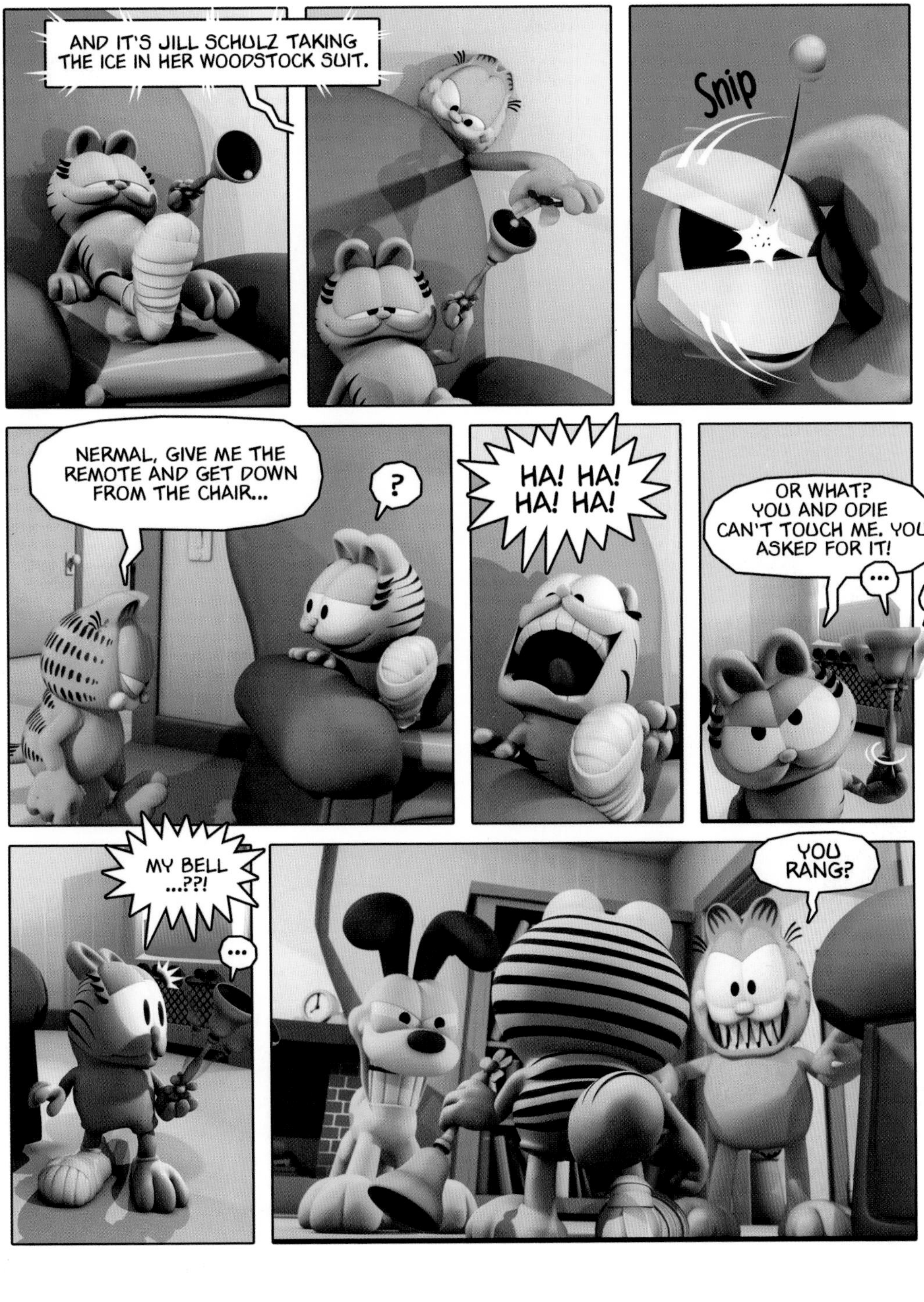
AND IT'S JILL SCHULZ TAKING THE ICE IN HER WOODSTOCK SUIT.
Snip
NERMAL, GIVE ME THE REMOTE AND GET DOWN FROM THE CHAIR...
?
HA! HA! HA! HA!
OR WHAT? YOU AND ODIE CAN'T TOUCH ME. YOU ASKED FOR IT!
...
...
MY BELL ...??!
...
YOU RANG?

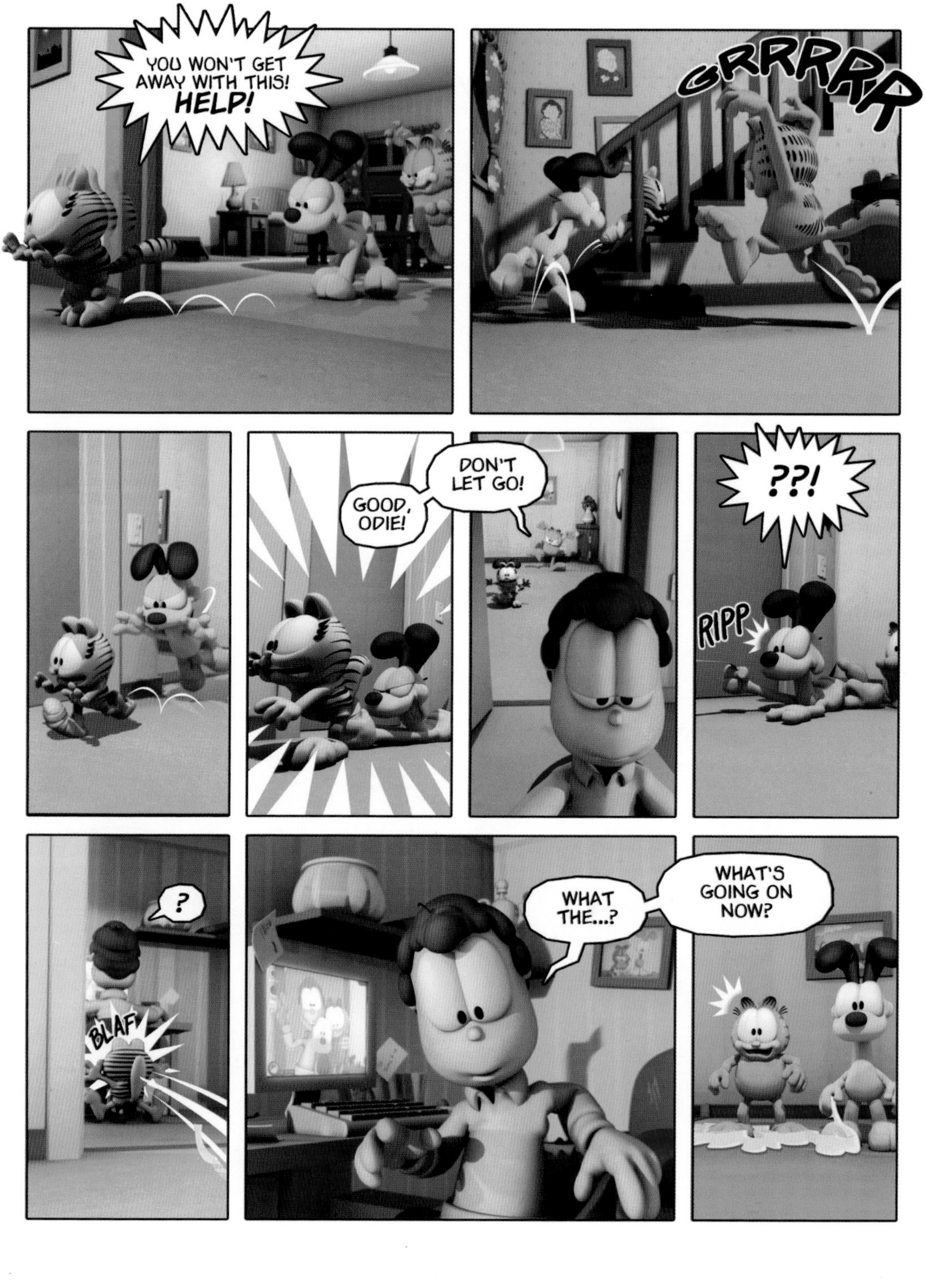
YOU WON'T GET AWAY WITH THIS! HELP!
GRRRRR
GOOD, ODIE!
DON'T LET GO!
??!
RIPP
?
BLAF!
WHAT THE...?
WHAT'S GOING ON NOW?

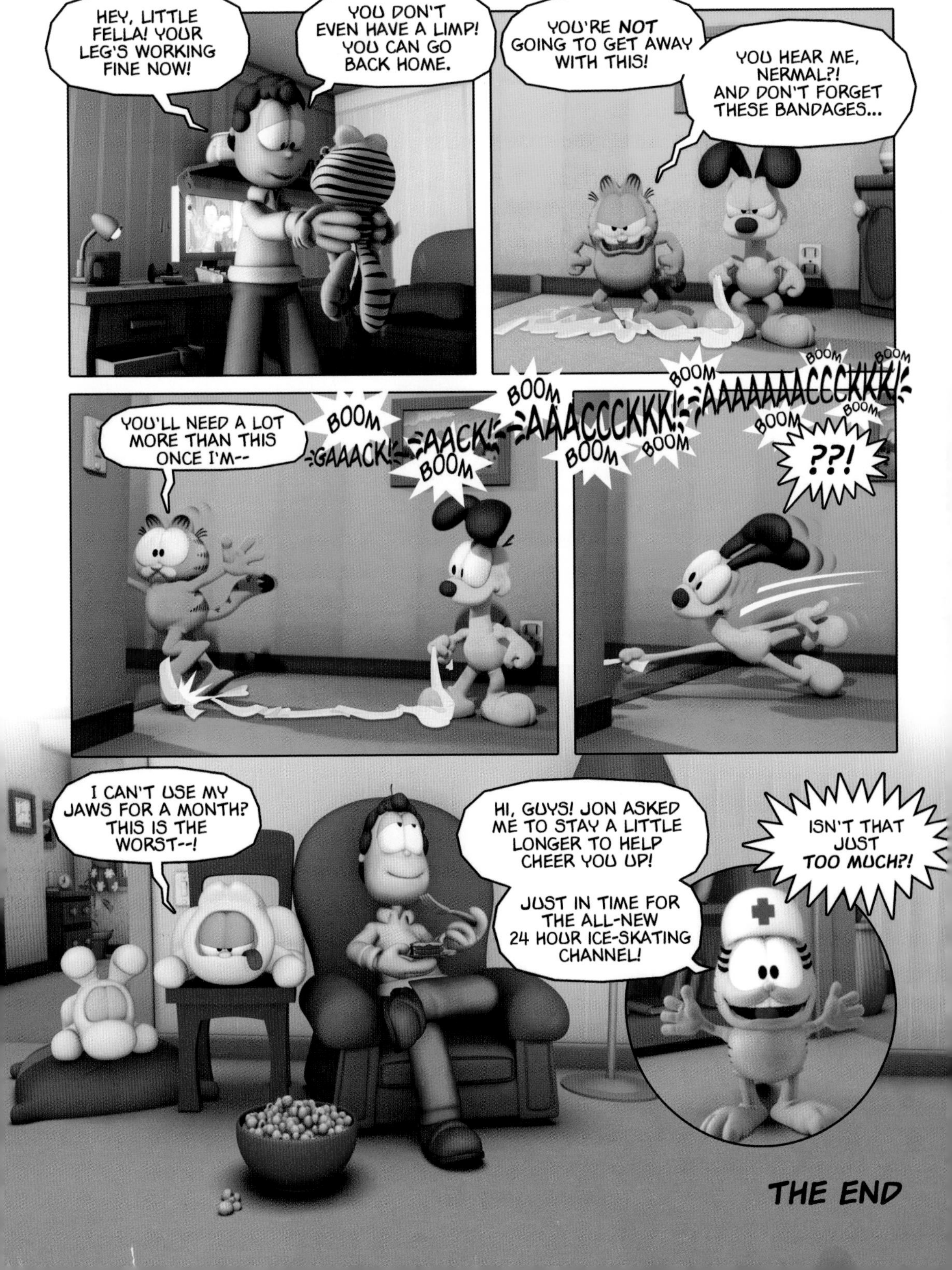
HEY, LITTLE FELLA! YOUR LEG'S WORKING FINE NOW!
YOU DON'T EVEN HAVE A LIMP! YOU CAN GO BACK HOME.
YOU'RE NOT GOING TO GET AWAY WITH THIS!
YOU HEAR ME, NERMAL?! AND DON'T FORGET THESE BANDAGES...
YOU'LL NEED A LOT MORE THAN THIS ONCE I'M--
BOOM
GAAACK!
AACK!
BOOM
BOOM
AAACCCKKK!
BOOM
BOOM
BOOM
AAAAAAACCCKKK!
BOOM
BOOM
BOOM
BOOM
??!
I CAN'T USE MY JAWS FOR A MONTH? THIS IS THE WORST--!
HI, GUYS! JON ASKED ME TO STAY A LITTLE LONGER TO HELP CHEER YOU UP!
JUST IN TIME FOR THE ALL-NEW 24 HOUR ICE-SKATING CHANNEL!
ISN'T THAT JUST TOO MUCH?!
THE END

WATCH OUT FOR PAPERCUTZ™

Welcome to the fattening fourth GARFIELD & Co graphic novel from Papercutz. I'm your Scrooge-like Editor-in-Chief, Jim Salicrup, with an extra-special holiday treat for you—a mini preview of an all-new Papercutz series available at booksellers everywhere—just in time for the holidays!

Just as we're thrilled to publish the orange, overweight, feline sensation, GARFIELD, created by cartoonist Jim Davis, and tiny blue folks, THE SMURFS, created by Peyo, we're equally excited to announce that we'll be publishing the MONSTER graphic novels by world-famous cartoonist Lewis Trondheim! It's the almost normal adventures of an almost ordinary family… with a pet monster. Here's a small excerpt from MONSTER #1 "Monster Christmas":

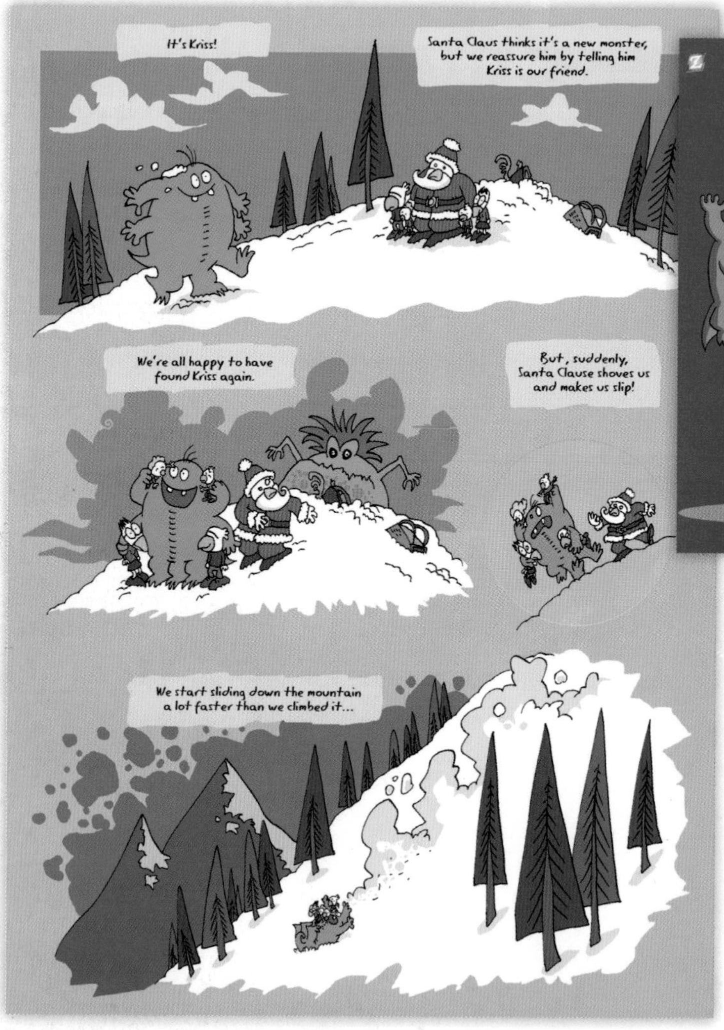
It's Kriss!
Santa Claus thinks it's a new monster, but we reassure him by telling him Kriss is our friend.
We're all happy to have found Kriss again.
But, suddenly, Santa Clause shoves us and makes us slip!
We start sliding down the mountain a lot faster than we climbed it…

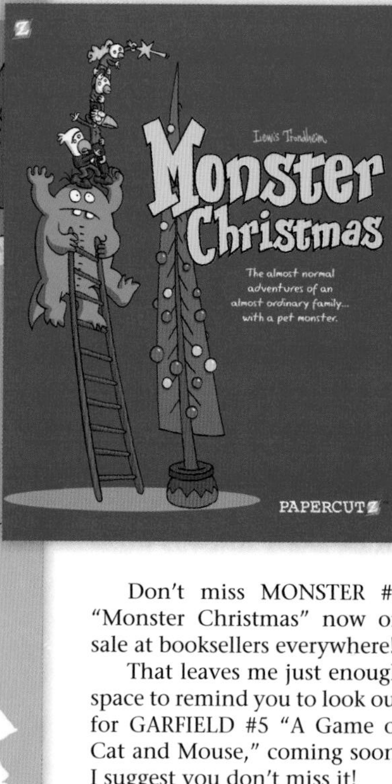
Lewis Trondheim
Monster Christmas
The almost normal adventures of an almost ordinary family… with a pet monster.
PAPERCUTZ

Don't miss MONSTER #1 "Monster Christmas" now on sale at booksellers everywhere!

That leaves me just enough space to remind you to look out for GARFIELD #5 "A Game of Cat and Mouse," coming soon. I suggest you don't miss it!

And most importantly, everyone at Papercutz wishes you the very best holiday season, and a happy and healthy New Year!

Jim

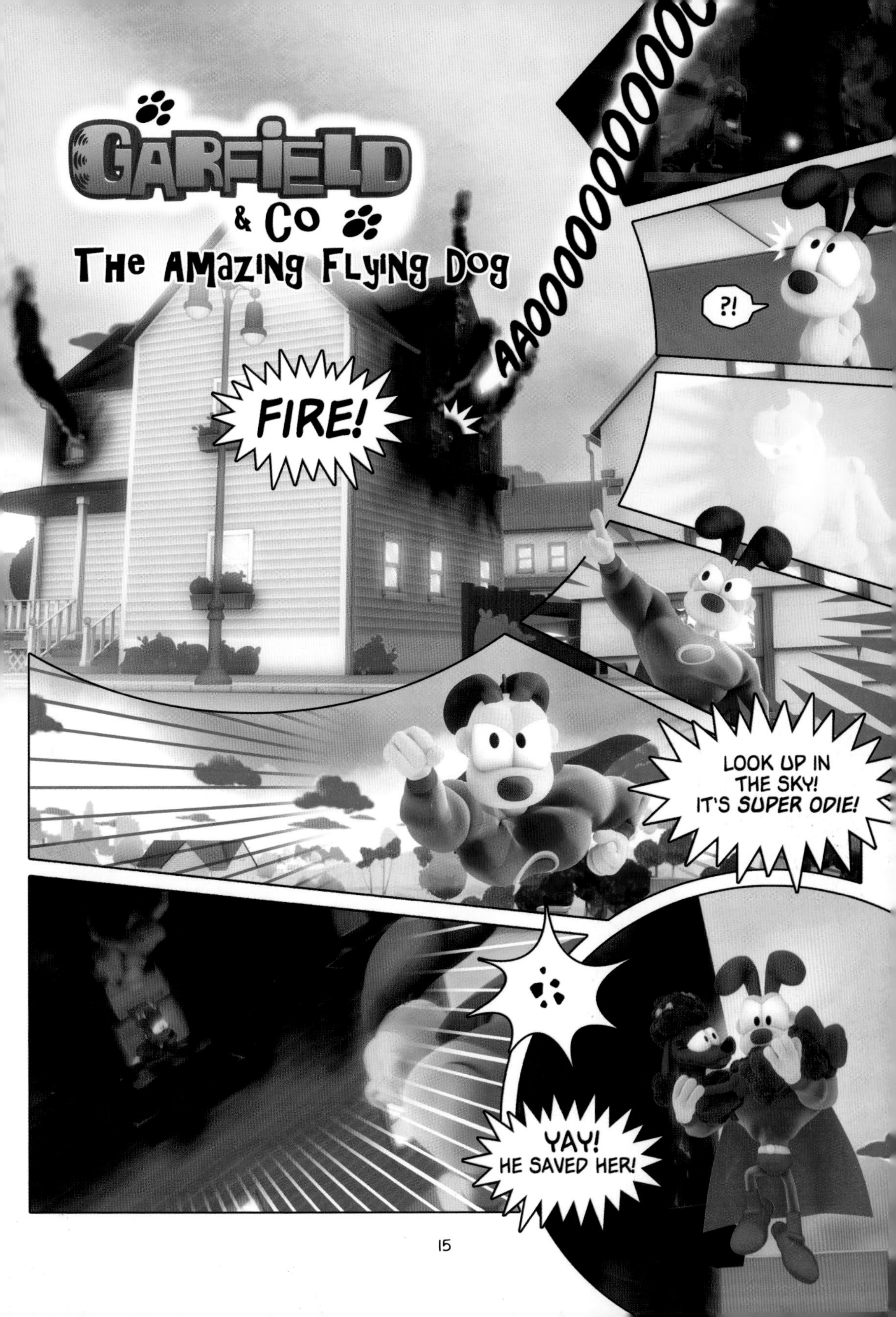

GARFIELD
& Co
The Amazing Flying Dog
FIRE!
AAOOOOOOOOOOO
?!
LOOK UP IN THE SKY! IT'S SUPER ODIE!
YAY! HE SAVED HER!

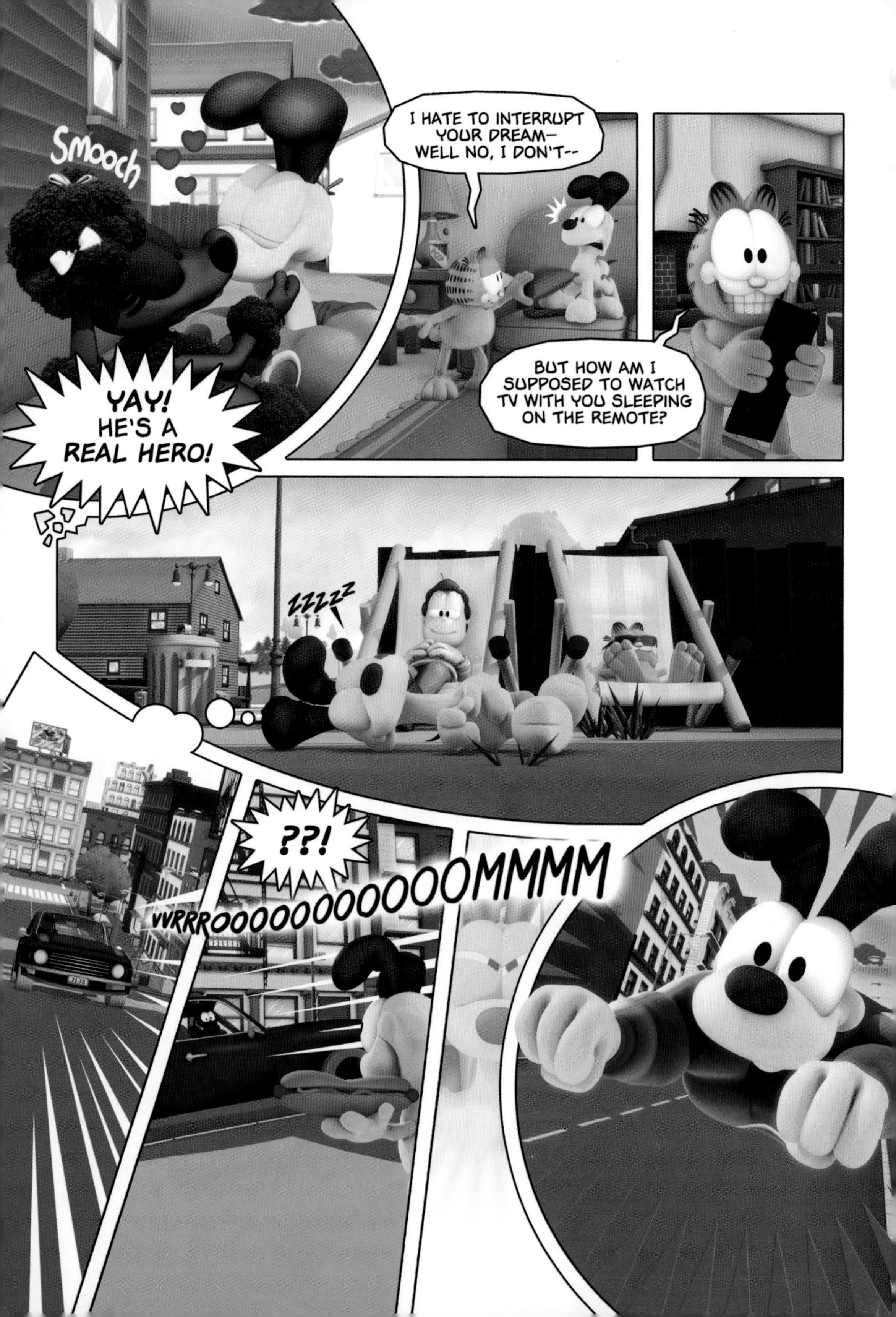

Smooch
YAY! HE'S A REAL HERO!
I HATE TO INTERRUPT YOUR DREAM— WELL NO, I DON'T--
BUT HOW AM I SUPPOSED TO WATCH TV WITH YOU SLEEPING ON THE REMOTE?
ZZZZZ
??!
VVRRROOOOOOOOOOOOMMMM

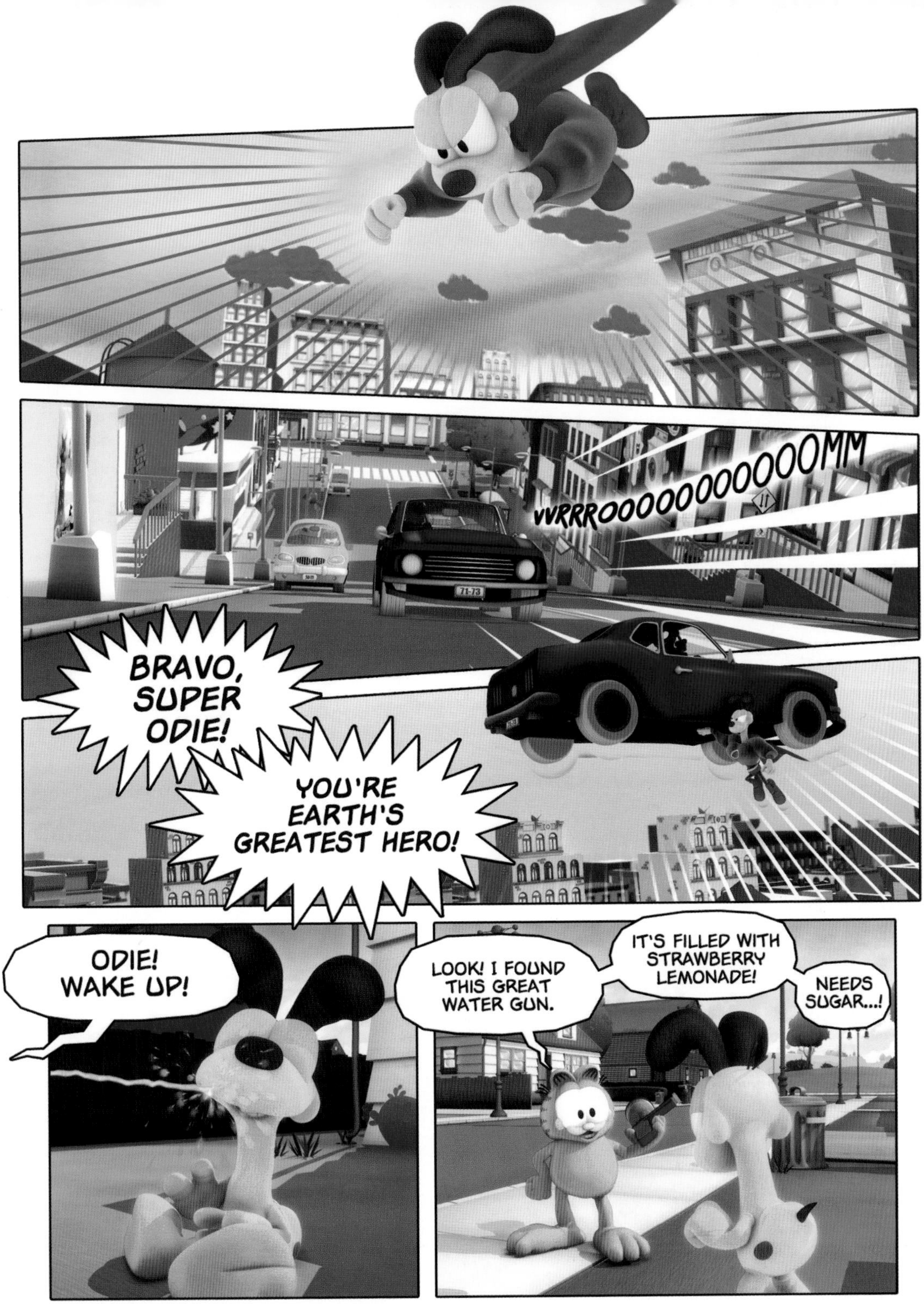
VVRRROOOOOOOOOOOMM
BRAVO, SUPER ODIE!
YOU'RE EARTH'S GREATEST HERO!
ODIE! WAKE UP!
LOOK! I FOUND THIS GREAT WATER GUN.
IT'S FILLED WITH STRAWBERRY LEMONADE!
NEEDS SUGAR...!

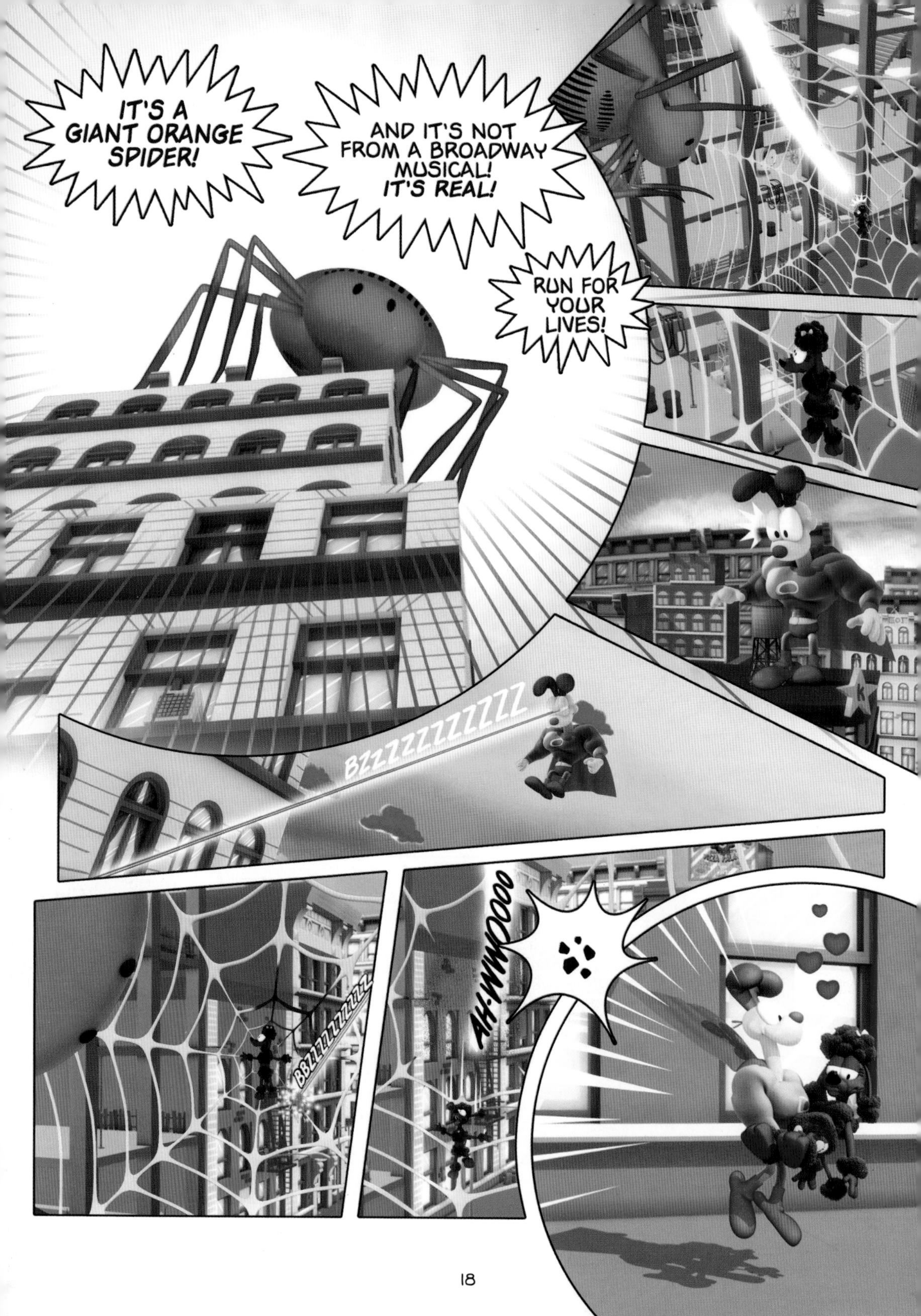
IT'S A GIANT ORANGE SPIDER!
AND IT'S NOT FROM A BROADWAY MUSICAL! IT'S REAL!
RUN FOR YOUR LIVES!
BZZZZZZZZZZZZ
BBZZZZZZZZZZ
AH-WWOOOO

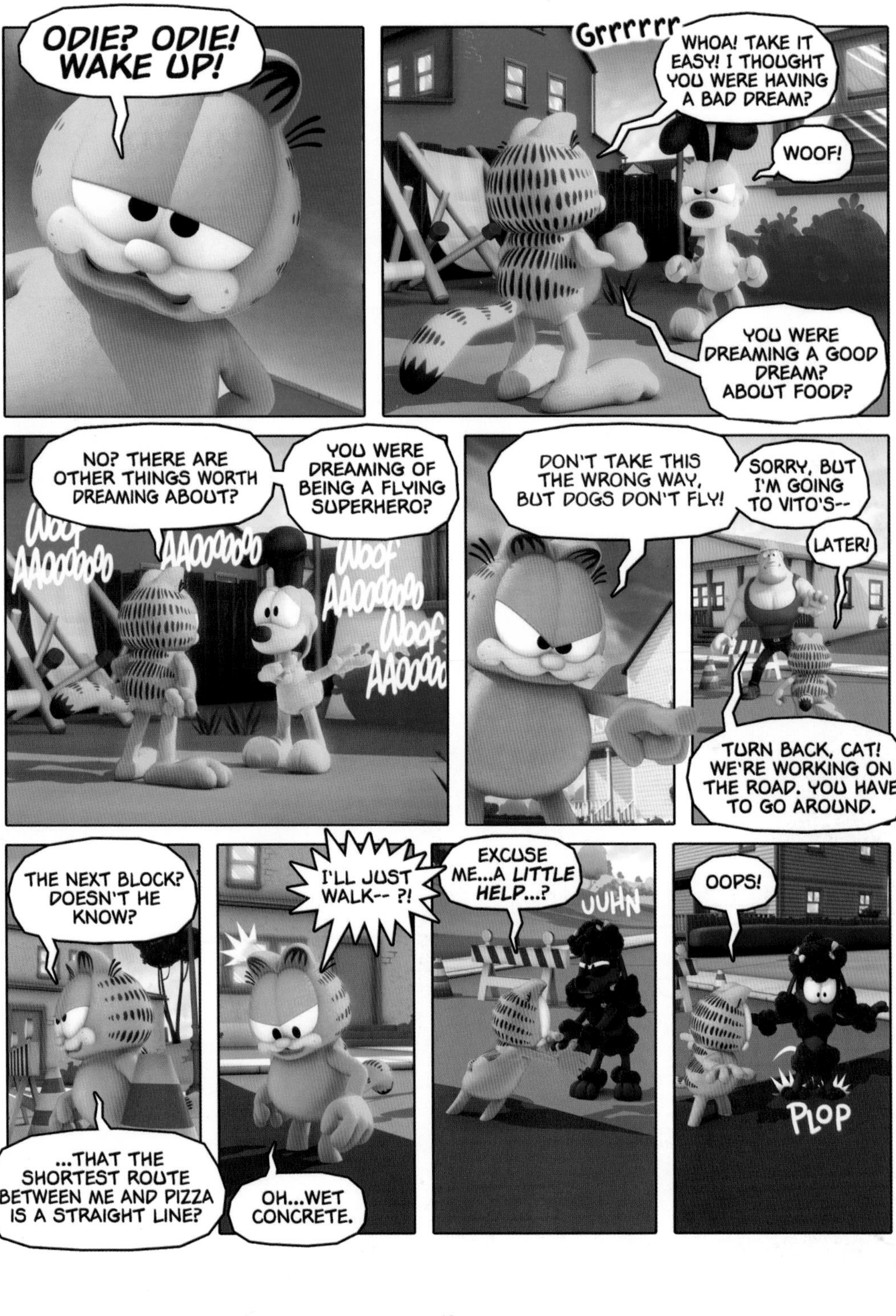
ODIE? ODIE! WAKE UP!
Grrrrrr
WHOA! TAKE IT EASY! I THOUGHT YOU WERE HAVING A BAD DREAM?
WOOF!
YOU WERE DREAMING A GOOD DREAM? ABOUT FOOD?
NO? THERE ARE OTHER THINGS WORTH DREAMING ABOUT?
YOU WERE DREAMING OF BEING A FLYING SUPERHERO?
Woof AAOOOOOOO
AAOOOOOOO
Woof AAOOOOOOO
Woof AAOOOOO
DON'T TAKE THIS THE WRONG WAY, BUT DOGS DON'T FLY!
SORRY, BUT I'M GOING TO VITO'S--
LATER!
TURN BACK, CAT! WE'RE WORKING ON THE ROAD. YOU HAVE TO GO AROUND.
THE NEXT BLOCK? DOESN'T HE KNOW?
...THAT THE SHORTEST ROUTE BETWEEN ME AND PIZZA IS A STRAIGHT LINE?
I'LL JUST WALK-- ?!
OH...WET CONCRETE.
EXCUSE ME...A LITTLE HELP...?
UUHN
OOPS!
PLOP

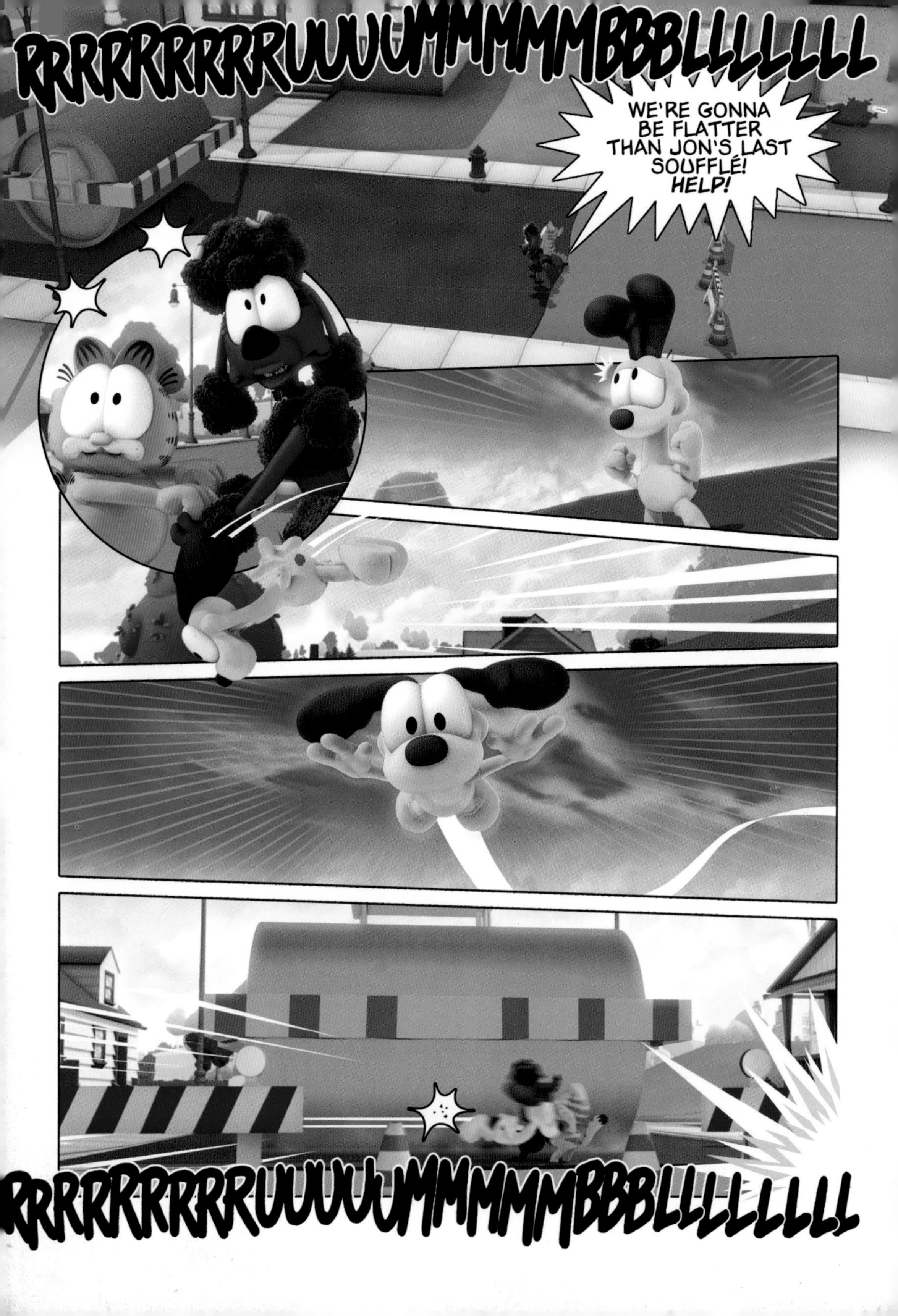
RRRRRRRRRRUUUUMMMMMMBBBLLLLLLL
WE'RE GONNA BE FLATTER THAN JON'S LAST SOUFFLÉ! HELP!
RRRRRRRRRRUUUUUMMMMMMBBBLLLLLLLL

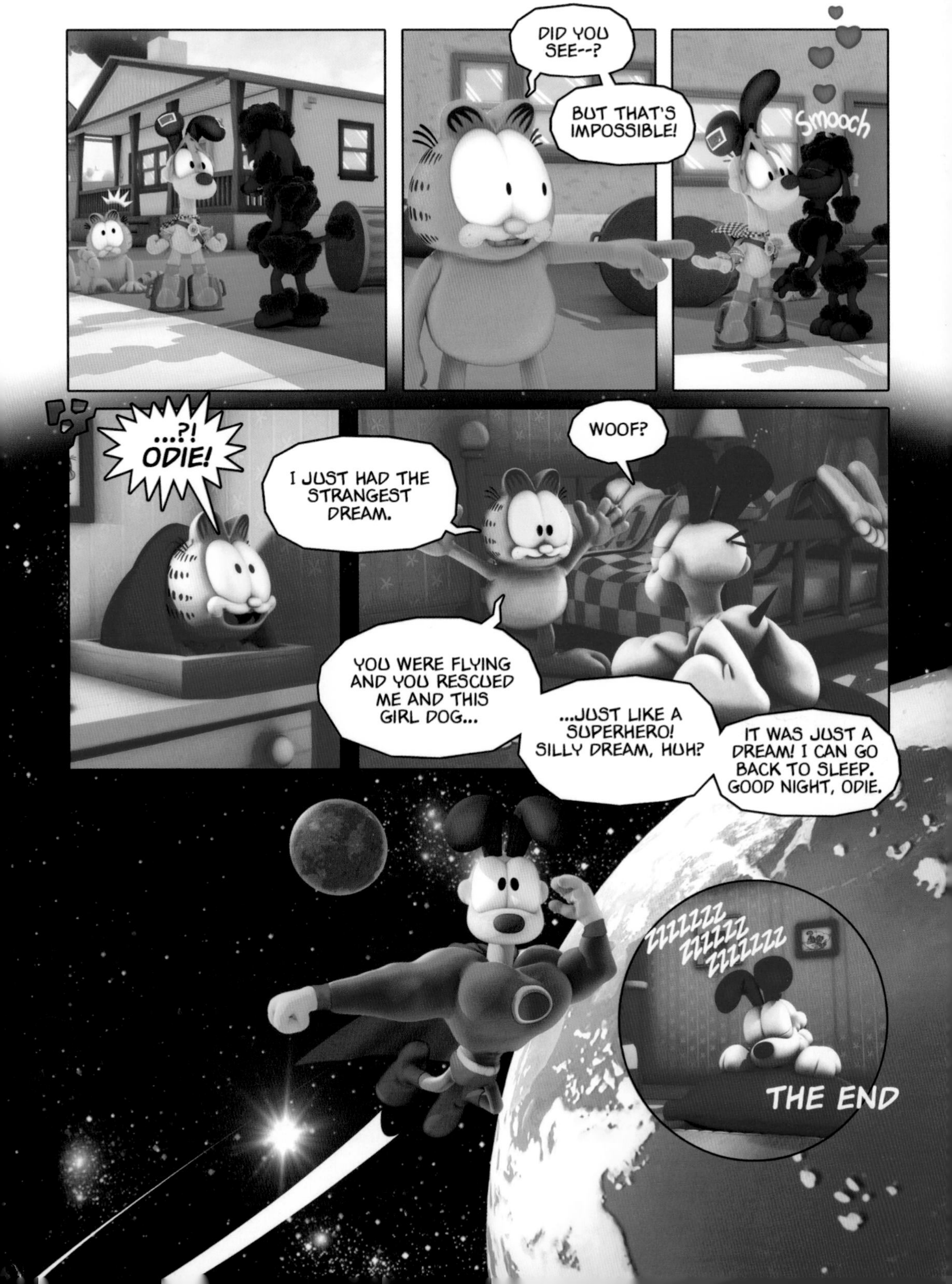
DID YOU SEE--?
BUT THAT'S IMPOSSIBLE!
Smooch
...?! ODIE!
I JUST HAD THE STRANGEST DREAM.
WOOF?
YOU WERE FLYING AND YOU RESCUED ME AND THIS GIRL DOG...
...JUST LIKE A SUPERHERO! SILLY DREAM, HUH?
IT WAS JUST A DREAM! I CAN GO BACK TO SLEEP. GOOD NIGHT, ODIE.
ZZZZZZZ ZZZZZZ ZZZZZZZ
THE END

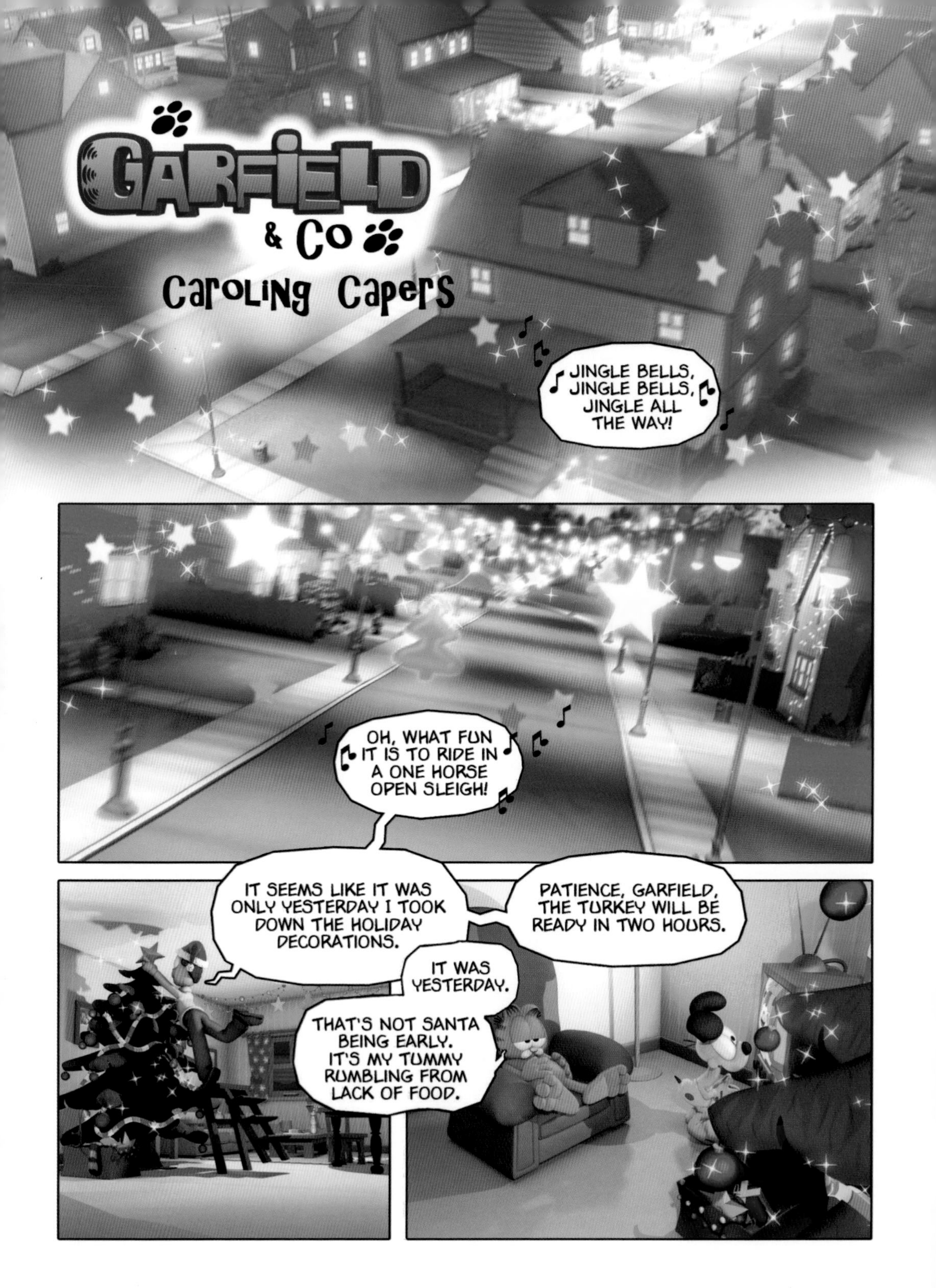
GARFIELD & Co
Caroling Capers
JINGLE BELLS, JINGLE BELLS, JINGLE ALL THE WAY!
OH, WHAT FUN IT IS TO RIDE IN A ONE HORSE OPEN SLEIGH!
IT SEEMS LIKE IT WAS ONLY YESTERDAY I TOOK DOWN THE HOLIDAY DECORATIONS.
IT WAS YESTERDAY.
PATIENCE, GARFIELD, THE TURKEY WILL BE READY IN TWO HOURS.
THAT'S NOT SANTA BEING EARLY. IT'S MY TUMMY RUMBLING FROM LACK OF FOOD.

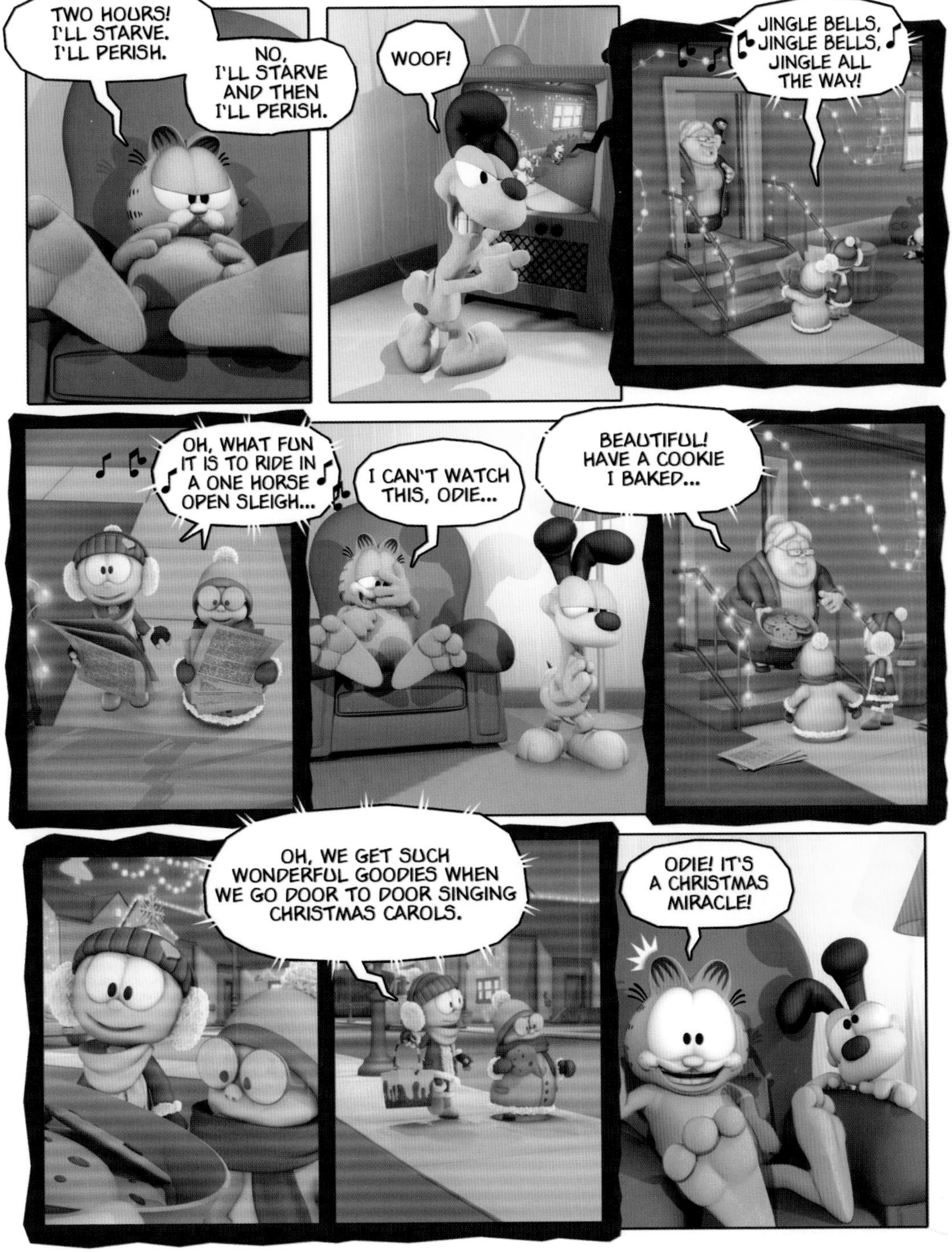
TWO HOURS! I'LL STARVE. I'LL PERISH.
NO, I'LL STARVE AND THEN I'LL PERISH.
WOOF!
JINGLE BELLS, JINGLE BELLS, JINGLE ALL THE WAY!
OH, WHAT FUN IT IS TO RIDE IN A ONE HORSE OPEN SLEIGH...
I CAN'T WATCH THIS, ODIE...
BEAUTIFUL! HAVE A COOKIE I BAKED...
OH, WE GET SUCH WONDERFUL GOODIES WHEN WE GO DOOR TO DOOR SINGING CHRISTMAS CAROLS.
ODIE! IT'S A CHRISTMAS MIRACLE!

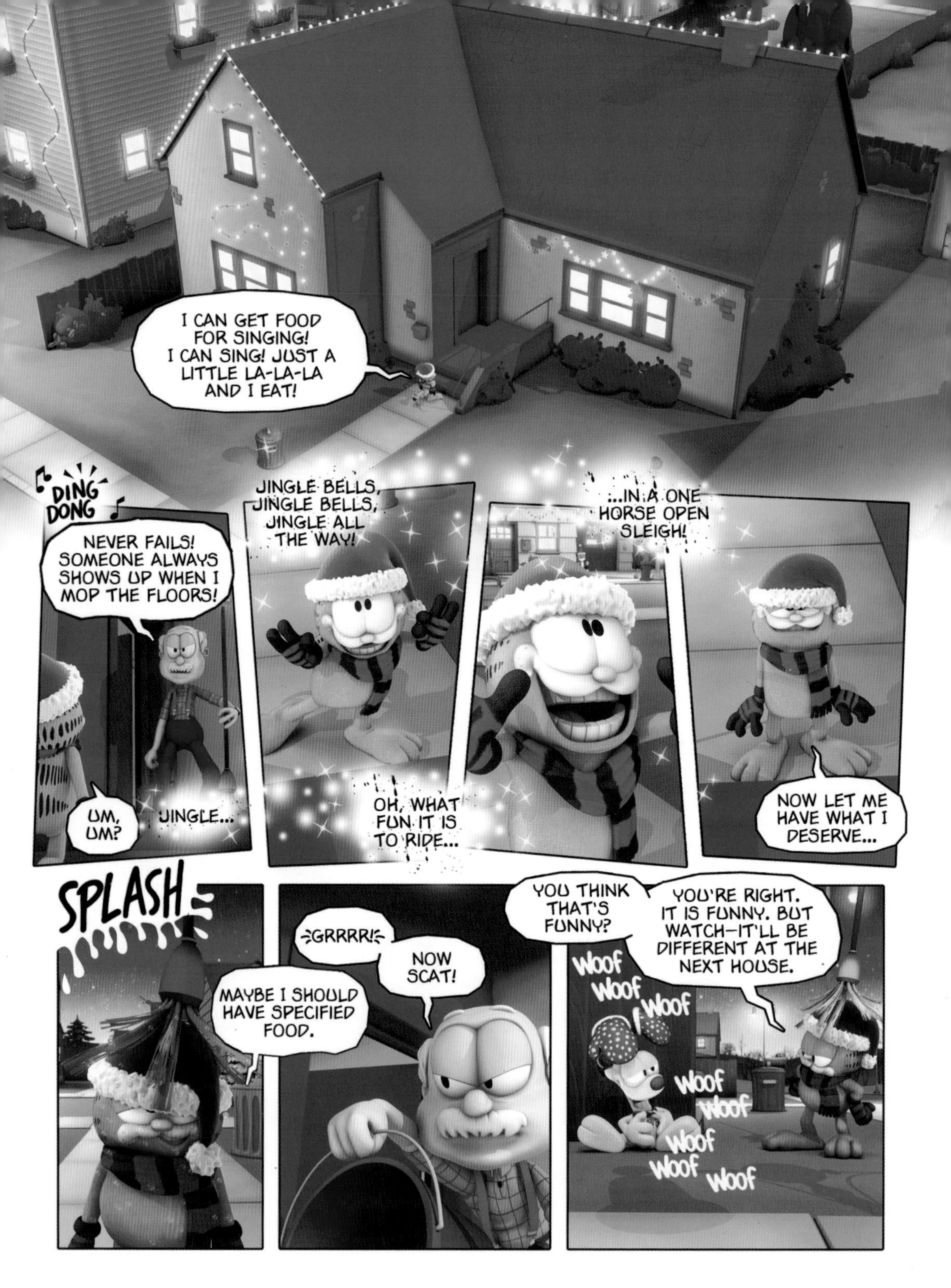
I CAN GET FOOD FOR SINGING! I CAN SING! JUST A LITTLE LA-LA-LA AND I EAT!
DING DONG
NEVER FAILS! SOMEONE ALWAYS SHOWS UP WHEN I MOP THE FLOORS!
UM, UM?
JINGLE...
JINGLE BELLS, JINGLE BELLS, JINGLE ALL THE WAY!
OH, WHAT FUN IT IS TO RIDE...
...IN A ONE HORSE OPEN SLEIGH!
NOW LET ME HAVE WHAT I DESERVE...
SPLASH
GRRRR!
NOW SCAT!
MAYBE I SHOULD HAVE SPECIFIED FOOD.
YOU THINK THAT'S FUNNY?
YOU'RE RIGHT. IT IS FUNNY. BUT WATCH—IT'LL BE DIFFERENT AT THE NEXT HOUSE.
Woof Woof Woof
Woof Woof Woof Woof Woof

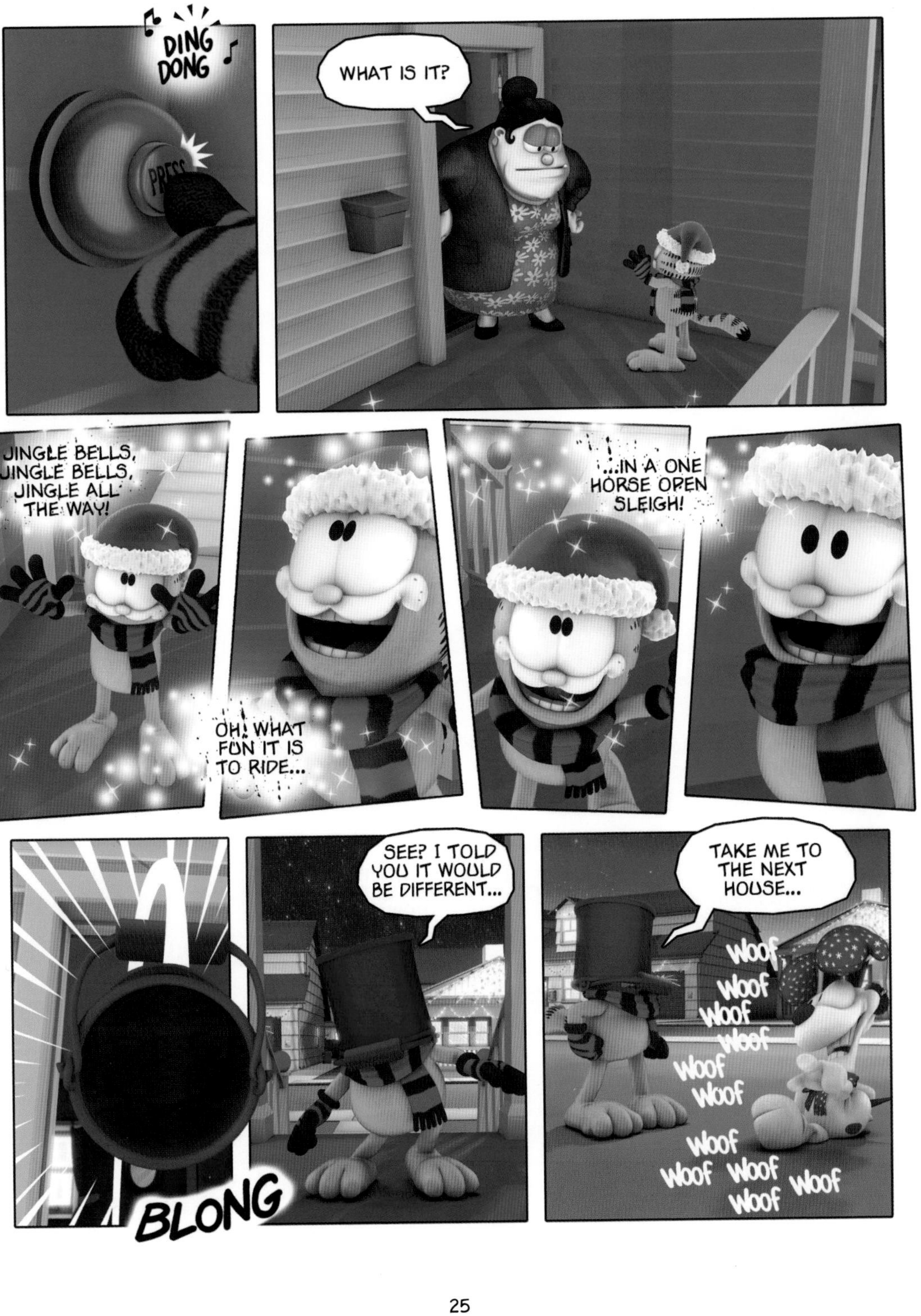
DING DONG
PRESS
WHAT IS IT?
JINGLE BELLS, JINGLE BELLS, JINGLE ALL THE WAY!
OH! WHAT FUN IT IS TO RIDE...
...IN A ONE HORSE OPEN SLEIGH!
BLONG
SEE? I TOLD YOU IT WOULD BE DIFFERENT...
TAKE ME TO THE NEXT HOUSE...
Woof Woof Woof Woof Woof Woof
Woof Woof Woof Woof Woof

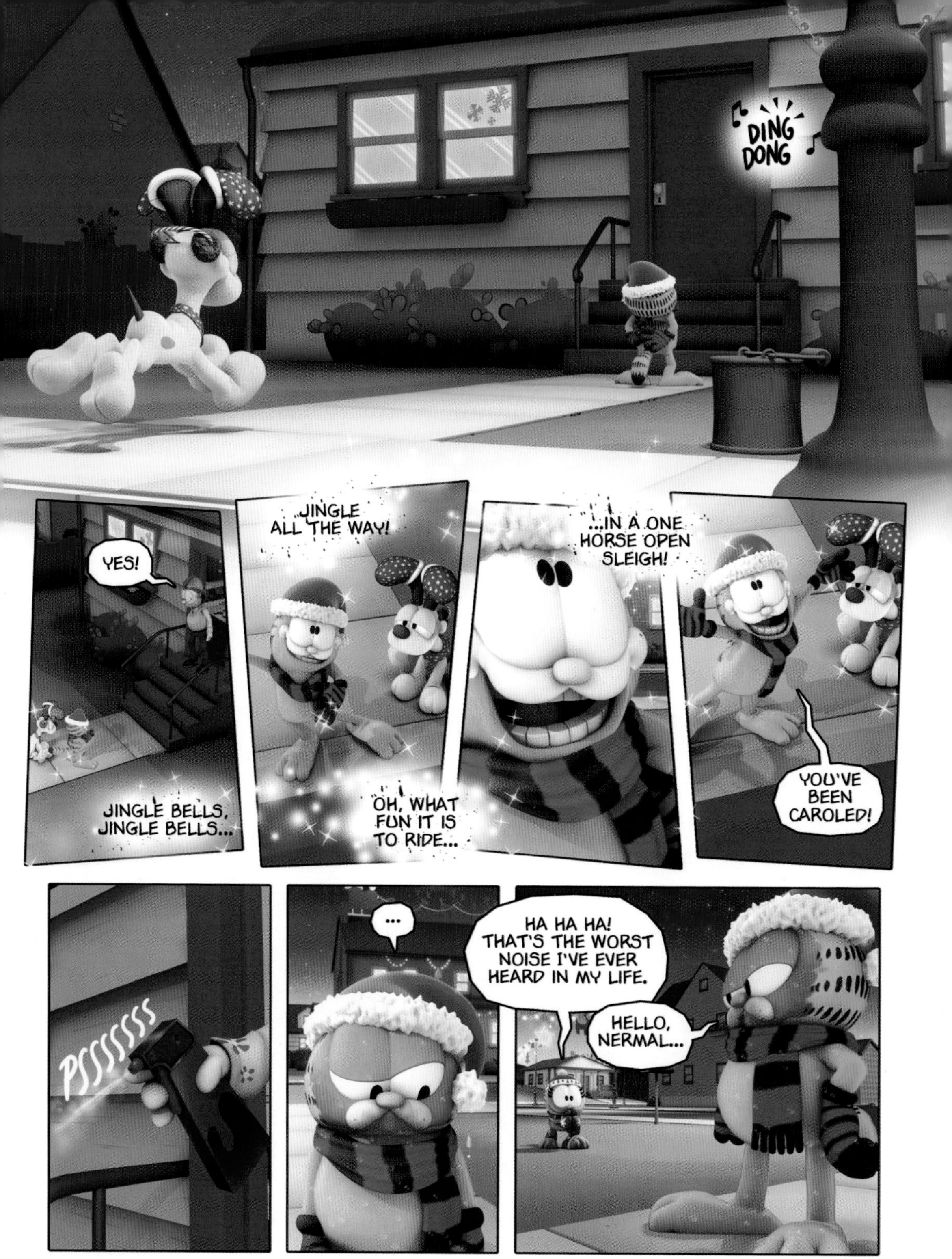
DING DONG
YES!
JINGLE BELLS, JINGLE BELLS...
JINGLE ALL THE WAY!
OH, WHAT FUN IT IS TO RIDE...
...IN A ONE HORSE OPEN SLEIGH!
YOU'VE BEEN CAROLED!
PSSSSSSS
...
HA HA HA! THAT'S THE WORST NOISE I'VE EVER HEARD IN MY LIFE.
HELLO, NERMAL...

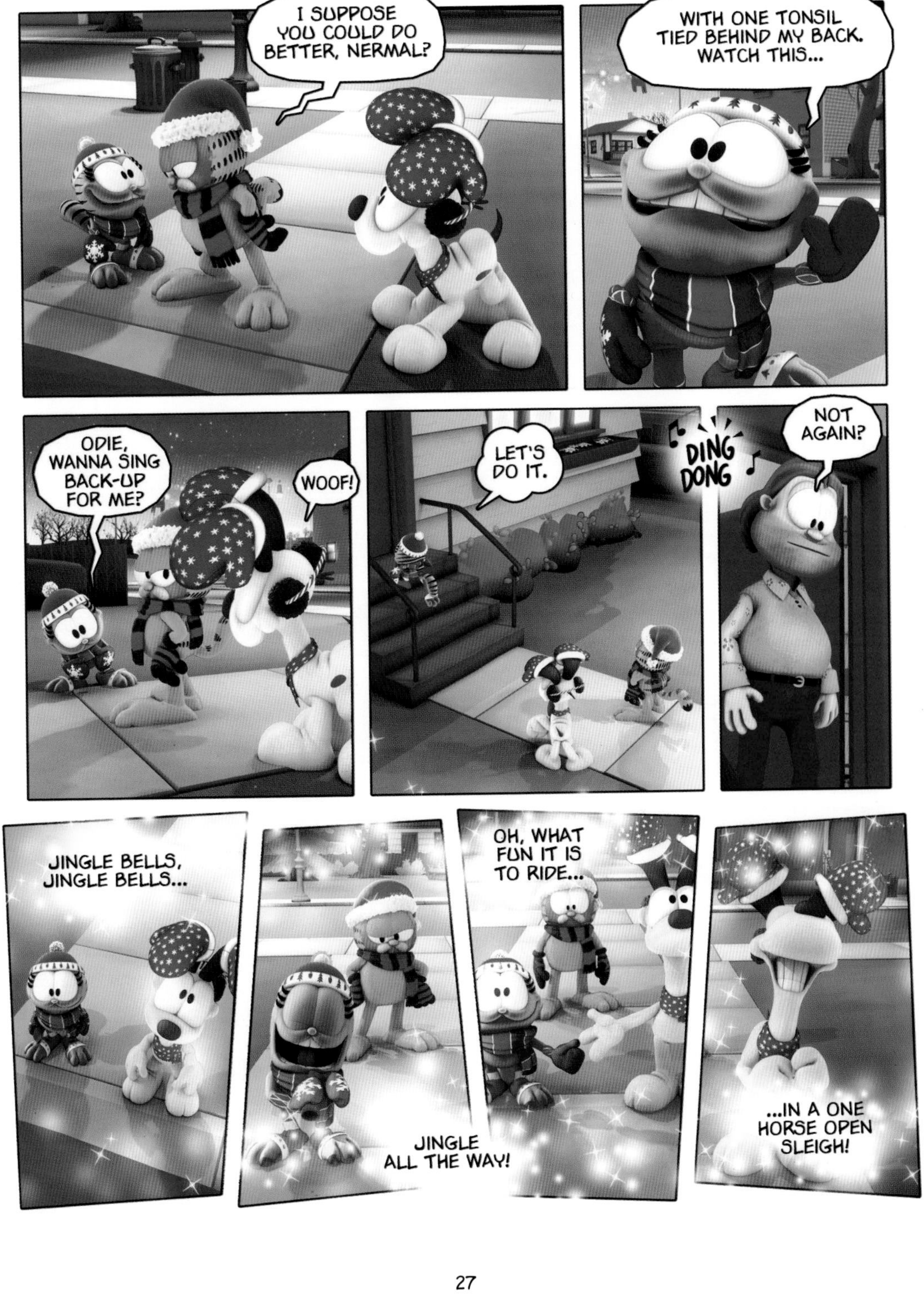
I SUPPOSE YOU COULD DO BETTER, NERMAL?
WITH ONE TONSIL TIED BEHIND MY BACK. WATCH THIS...
ODIE, WANNA SING BACK-UP FOR ME?
WOOF!
LET'S DO IT.
DING DONG
NOT AGAIN?
JINGLE BELLS, JINGLE BELLS...
JINGLE ALL THE WAY!
OH, WHAT FUN IT IS TO RIDE...
...IN A ONE HORSE OPEN SLEIGH!

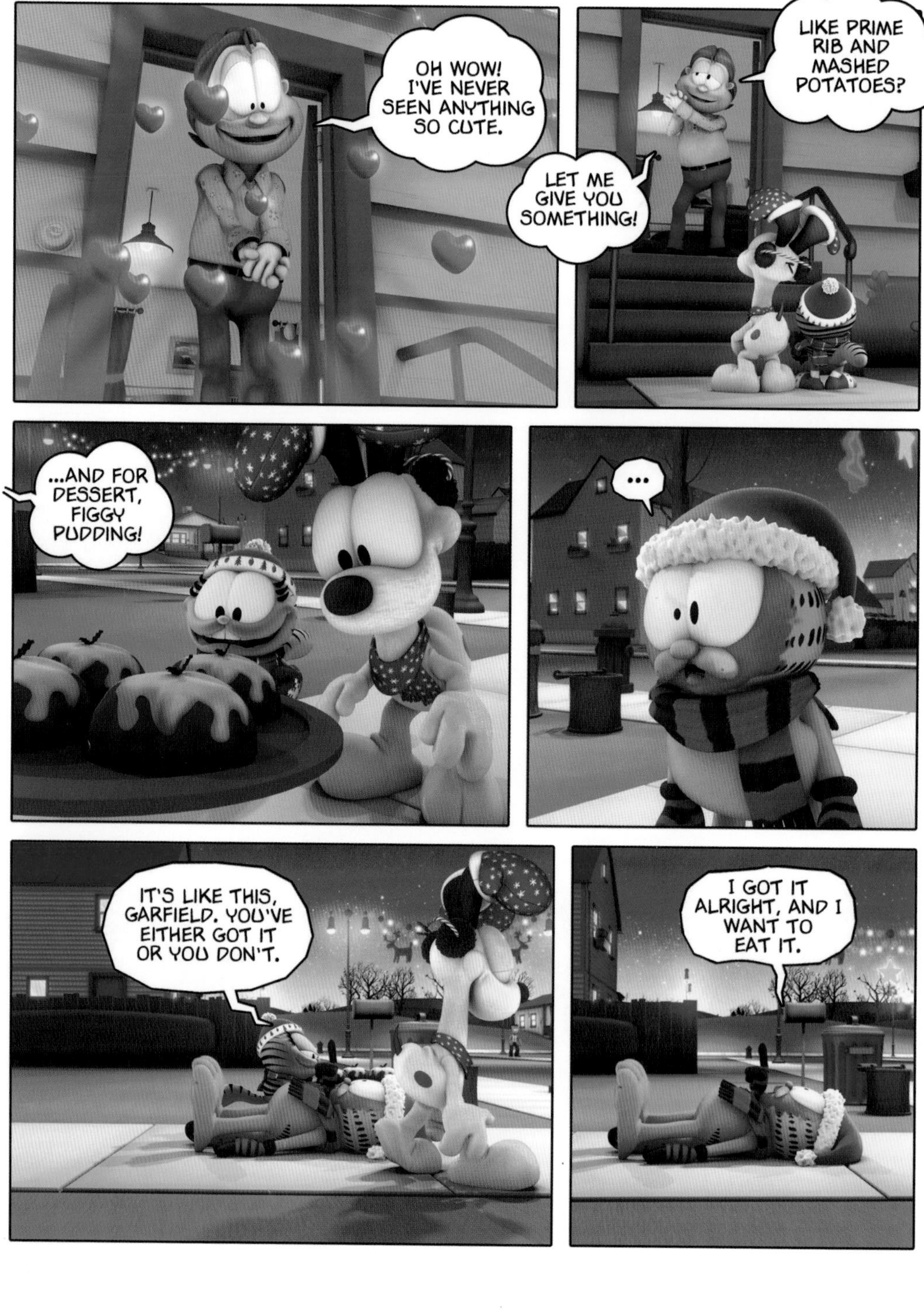
OH WOW! I'VE NEVER SEEN ANYTHING SO CUTE.
LIKE PRIME RIB AND MASHED POTATOES?
LET ME GIVE YOU SOMETHING!
...AND FOR DESSERT, FIGGY PUDDING!
...
IT'S LIKE THIS, GARFIELD. YOU'VE EITHER GOT IT OR YOU DON'T.
I GOT IT ALRIGHT, AND I WANT TO EAT IT.

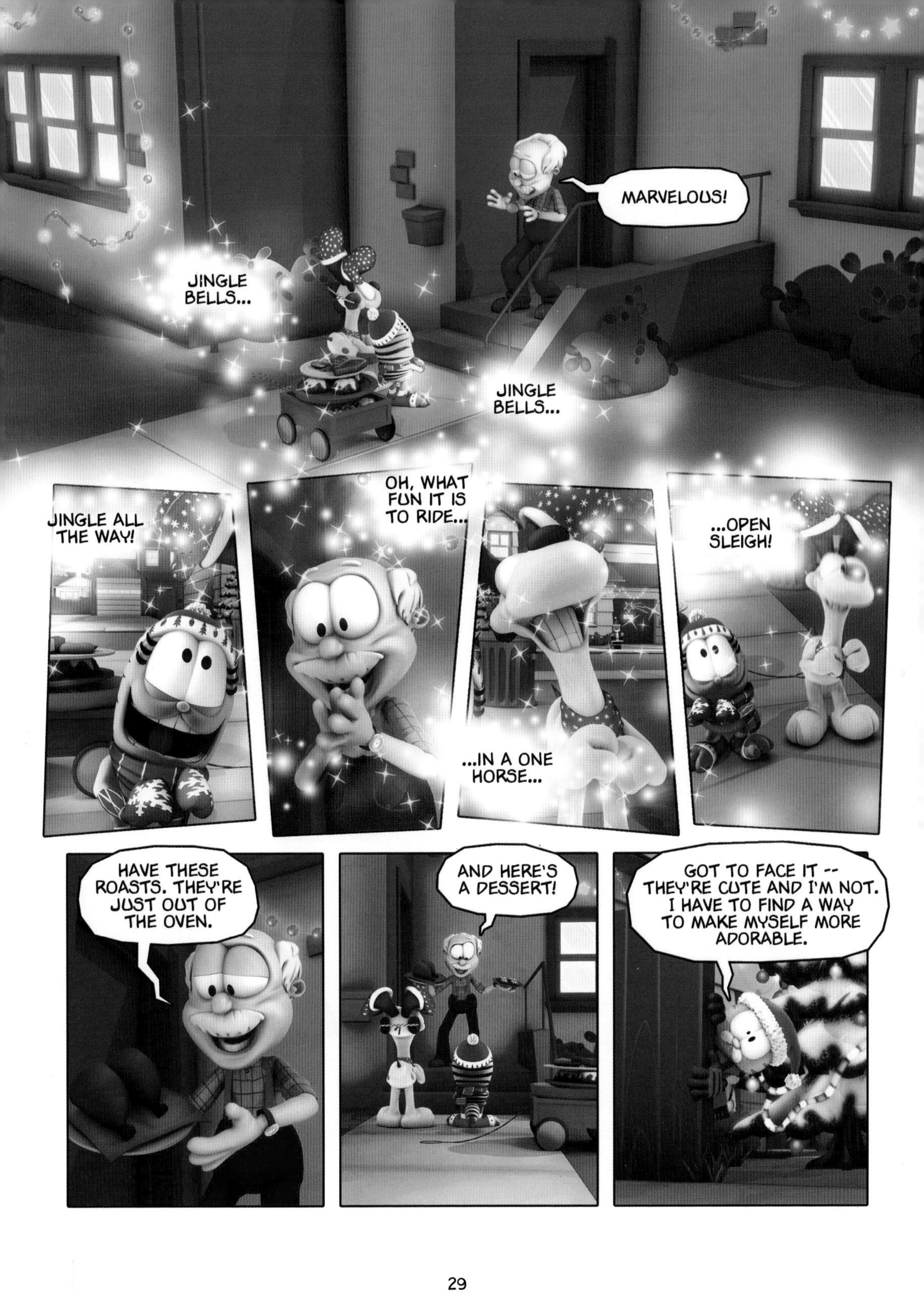
MARVELOUS!
JINGLE BELLS...
JINGLE BELLS...
JINGLE ALL THE WAY!
OH, WHAT FUN IT IS TO RIDE...
...IN A ONE HORSE...
...OPEN SLEIGH!
HAVE THESE ROASTS. THEY'RE JUST OUT OF THE OVEN.
AND HERE'S A DESSERT!
GOT TO FACE IT -- THEY'RE CUTE AND I'M NOT. I HAVE TO FIND A WAY TO MAKE MYSELF MORE ADORABLE.

IT'S NO USE.

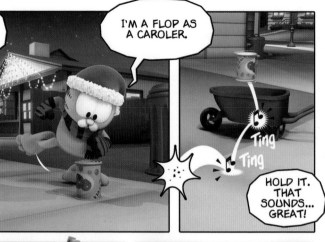

I'M A FLOP AS A CAROLER.

Ting
Ting

HOLD IT. THAT SOUNDS... GREAT!

TOO BAD I CAN'T HIT NOTES LIKE THAT.

WAIT A SECOND. MAYBE I CAN...

Blang
Blong
Bling

HEY! THAT'S NOT BAD!

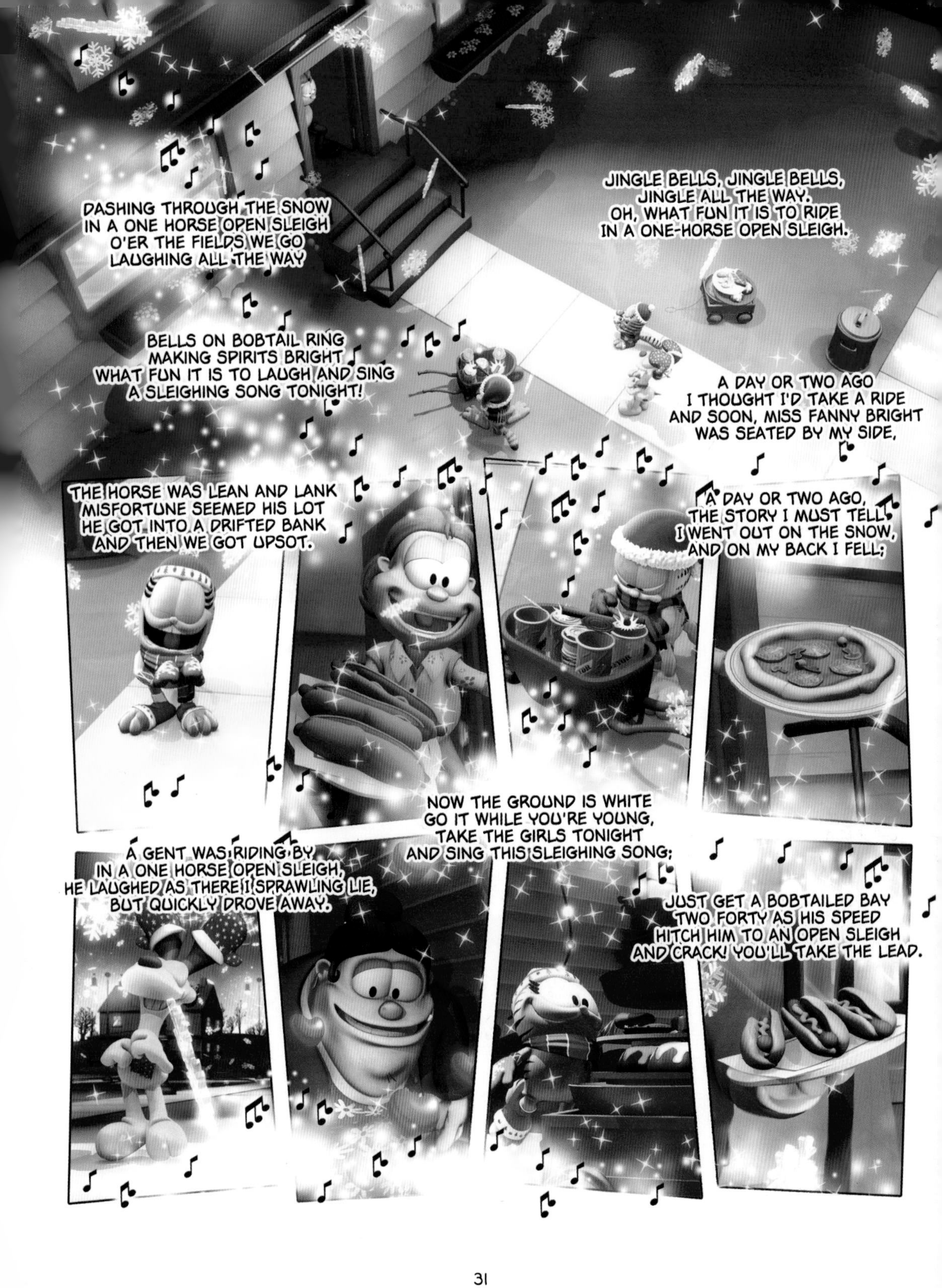
DASHING THROUGH THE SNOW IN A ONE HORSE OPEN SLEIGH O'ER THE FIELDS WE GO LAUGHING ALL THE WAY
JINGLE BELLS, JINGLE BELLS, JINGLE ALL THE WAY. OH, WHAT FUN IT IS TO RIDE IN A ONE-HORSE OPEN SLEIGH.
BELLS ON BOBTAIL RING MAKING SPIRITS BRIGHT WHAT FUN IT IS TO LAUGH AND SING A SLEIGHING SONG TONIGHT!
A DAY OR TWO AGO I THOUGHT I'D TAKE A RIDE AND SOON, MISS FANNY BRIGHT WAS SEATED BY MY SIDE,
THE HORSE WAS LEAN AND LANK MISFORTUNE SEEMED HIS LOT HE GOT INTO A DRIFTED BANK AND THEN WE GOT UPSOT.
A DAY OR TWO AGO, THE STORY I MUST TELL I WENT OUT ON THE SNOW, AND ON MY BACK I FELL;
A GENT WAS RIDING BY, IN A ONE HORSE OPEN SLEIGH, HE LAUGHED AS THERE I SPRAWLING LIE, BUT QUICKLY DROVE AWAY.
NOW THE GROUND IS WHITE GO IT WHILE YOU'RE YOUNG, TAKE THE GIRLS TONIGHT AND SING THIS SLEIGHING SONG;
JUST GET A BOBTAILED BAY TWO FORTY AS HIS SPEED HITCH HIM TO AN OPEN SLEIGH AND CRACK! YOU'LL TAKE THE LEAD.